THE EXPERT

A Sixties Mystery

BERNARD KNIGHT

First published by Sphere Books Ltd 1976 (hardback)
Published by Robert Hale Ltd 1977 (paperback)
This edition published by Accent Press 2016

ISBN 9781910939895

Author's note

The Sixties Mysteries is a series of reissues of my early crime stories, the first of which was originally published in 1963. Looking back now, it is evident how criminal investigation has changed over the last half-century. Though basic police procedure is broadly the same, in these pages you will find no Crime Scene Managers or Crown Prosecution Service, no DNA, CSI, PACE, nor any of the other acronyms beloved of modern novels and television. These were the days when detectives still wore belted raincoats and trilby hats. There was no Health and Safety to plague us and the police smoked and drank tea alongside the post-mortem table!

Modern juries are now more interested in the reports of the forensic laboratory than in the diligent labours of the humble detective, though it is still the latter that solves most serious crimes. This is not to by any means belittle the enormous advances made in forensic science in recent years, but to serve as a reminder that the old murder teams did a pretty good job based simply on experience and dogged investigation.

Bernard Knight
2015

Prologue

The blonde was slightly drunk. She giggled and swayed a little as the man put an arm around her shoulders. They left the car and went inside.

She still clutched the few fivers that he had pressed on her during the ride.

'I'm not that sort of girl,' she had said, but she gave a silly little laugh and made no move to hand them back.

'Buy yourself some new undies,' he said. 'You'll probably need them by the time I've finished with you.'

He whispered something in her ear as they jostled up the stairs. She sniggered and bumped him playfully with her shoulder.

In the bedroom, he pulled off her coat and threw it carelessly at a chair. It missed and fell to the floor.

Grabbing her roughly, he pushed her back on to the bed and dropped heavily on top of her, kissing her greedily.

'Hey, mister, don't eat me!'

She had stopped giggling now.

Still holding her tightly, he put his mouth to her ear. 'I've been nice to you. Are you going to be nice to me?'

She tried to focus her eyes close enough to see his face. The first doubts about him began to filter into her fuddled mind.

He kissed her again, savagely. With his lips back at her ear, he whispered something again.

Immediately she tried to struggle back to a sitting position.

'No damn fear, I won't,' she said thickly. 'Let go of me, you bloody nutter!'

He kissed her even more violently this time, pushing her head down against the bedcover.

'Come on, don't play pure and simple with me. You've been around, girlie!'

She started to yell, but he clapped a hand across her face. With the other hand he reached out to grope in the drawer of the bedside table.

Chapter One

The shrill sound of the telephone ravaged the quietness of the empty study. Its double peal clawed harshly at the darkness for minute after long minute. Whoever was on the other end was hell-bent on getting an answer.

Outside the study, the hall was dark, except for a thin shaft of weak moonlight that poked its way through the landing window. The deep tick of a grandfather clock seemed disdainful of the raucous jangle from the other room.

Suddenly, a door opened upstairs and brighter light flooded the landing. Muttering under his breath, John Hardy pulled the cord of a red brocade dressing gown about him, as he padded down the stairs into the gloom below.

The familiarity of years guided him accurately to the study door. He pressed the light switch and hurried to the noisy phone that sat on his big mahogany desk.

'Hello, Doctor Hardy here.'

He listened for a moment, then slid onto the desk, his slippered feet dangling just above the carpet.

'Yes, I'm sorry about that. I'd forgotten to switch it through to the bedroom extension. Been away so long I'd lost the habit.'

He listened again, then looked sharply up at the electric clock above a bookcase.

'I make it twelve minutes past midnight now. If I come up the main road as far as Five Ways, can you have a car waiting there to pilot me through those small roads? I don't know them all that well, especially in the dark.'

The receiver croaked again into his ear and he nodded, as if the caller could see him.

'That's fine, then. I'll be in a beige Range Rover. Say twenty minutes time. I've got to get some clothes on first.'

He dropped the telephone delicately into its cradle and sighed. Life went on just the same – and so, it seemed, did death.

Turning out the light, he went back up the stairs, listening with distaste to a distant rumble of thunder. 'Duck boots and a mac,' he murmured. He went back into his bedroom and cast a longing glance at the open book lying on his bedside table. Then his eyes strayed to the big double bed, only one side of which was rumpled.

A sudden unwelcome lump came into his throat, followed quickly by a feeling of near terror. He had realised that this was the first call since that awful one almost three months ago.

Hardy stared at the bed, almost hypnotised, illogical panic sweeping over him.

It passed as quickly as it had come and he took a deep breath and straightened up.

'For God's sake, don't be so damned self-pitying,' he said loudly.

He marched through into a small dressing room and peeled off his night things. Running a quick hand over his chin, he decided that his morning shave would have to last. Then he selected a check sports shirt and a thick jumper from a drawer under a wardrobe. Thick socks and a pair of old golfing trousers went on over his underpants and, in a few moments, he was ready for action. Another peal of thunder, nearer this time, sent him groping on top of a cupboard for a waterproof trilby that still had little tears in the crown from fishing flies.

He picked up his watch and wallet and padded down the stairs of the silent house. This time, he went through the kitchen to his laboratory, which had been closed up for ten weeks and smelt dusty and stale.

On a table near a window was his square, black doctor's bag. He swung it off, hoping that Sandra, his last laboratory technician, had topped it up before she left for her new job in Liverpool.

Hardy went back into the kitchen and opened the door into the garden. He stepped out on to the gravel path and, looking up, saw that black clouds were rolling across the pale moon. Again a grumble of thunder came from the west. He had taken a fishing jacket from the hall on his way out and now he paused to struggle into it, as the first drops of rain started to tap tentatively on the garage roof.

The coat was of a thick olive-green nylon and again a flash of morbid recollection hit him, as he remembered that he had last worn it when Jo had been shot.

He ground his teeth at the vexation of discovering that John Hardy was not the impassive, coldly logical man he held himself to be. Stamping across the crunchy gravel to the garage, he deliberately put these thoughts from his mind, as he went in and groped for the light switch.

He put the bag into the back of the Rover, then picked a pair of wellington boots from the floor and dropped them in alongside the bag. They would be cold and possibly damp, but there was nothing he could do about it. From the description Carrol had given over the phone, he was going to need them, damp or not. Hardy lifted the roller door and switched off the light.

The car started at the first touch and he drove away, not bothering to close the door after him.

His headlights carved a swathe out of the night as he went towards the A41 trunk road that led from Warwick to Birmingham. The Rover was on loan from a dealer, so at least there were no painful memories attached to that. His white Alfa Romeo had been accidentally destroyed by fire when he was away, while having a routine service done in the dealer's premises. Until the insurance company decided what was to happen about a replacement, he had been loaned this one by a highly apologetic manager.

Hardy set the car's nose northwards, with about eight miles to the rendezvous with the police. It was not yet half past twelve, but the roads were very quiet. The threatening weather, now with flashes of lightning and frequent thunderclaps, was keeping all but the most determined people at home.

Then the rain came swishing down and Hardy groaned at the thought of the next couple of hours. After twenty-five years at the game he knew that most of the investigation at the scene would consist of waiting ... waiting for the photographer, waiting for the lighting, waiting for the forensic lab, waiting for the undertaker. *And looking at the weather now, maybe even waiting for frogmen*, he thought cynically.

All that the CID chief had told him on the phone was that a girl's body had been found in a disused quarry deep in a wood. The place was near some remote hamlet in the countryside, within the triangle formed by Warwick, Birmingham and Stratford-upon-Avon. He had no other details, but he knew Carrol of old and if Carrol said, 'It's a nasty one, Doc,' then that was good enough. If it had been a younger and less senior detective, then Hardy might have wanted a few more details before turning out so promptly into a filthy night like this, but Carrol's laconic description was a warranty of the seriousness of the case.

John Hardy wondered, as he peered down the bright tunnel of his headlights, just how many times he had driven off into the unknown like this. How many black nights and grey dawns had he seen, standing with a posse of big, grave men over some pathetic or horrifying scene of violent death? He sometimes wondered at times like these why on earth he had ever chosen forensic pathology – surely the most macabre, as well as the least popular career in medicine. He never seemed to be called to a murder at eleven o'clock on a sunny Tuesday morning. It was always – in his memory at least – between midnight and four in the morning, always cold, usually raining or snowing. It was always with a full day's engagements ahead of him – that needed a dozen frantic telephone calls to rearrange. Either that or he was about to catch the ferry to a holiday on the continent or an aeroplane to some conference in America.

As he watched the big raindrops flying at him down the light beams, he suddenly realised that he was getting old and crabby. Thank God that he had some insight left, he thought, mentally shaking himself out of his introspective, self-indulgent mood. This was surely the most interesting job in the world. He was privileged to be doing it and wouldn't think of changing it for any inducement on earth.

But it isn't the same any more, he thought, his shoulders sagging again. Jo had gone.

He tried to tell himself that it wasn't just that, but deep down, he knew it was true. The fire had gone out of his belly – or if it hadn't gone, it was burning pretty low.

This first call after his return showed him that three months and a trip halfway round the world had made little difference to the acutely depressed person that he had been immediately after the death of his wife.

This night was going to be a test, he knew that.

Like the man who goes back into the water after almost drowning or the air pilot who flies again after his crash, this was to be the make-or-break case.

He sat upright again, quickly.

'Balderdash! John Hardy, you damned sentimental, cringing worm! Snap out of it!'

After a pause, he added loudly, 'And stop damn well talking to yourself!'

He felt better after this and settled down to concentrate on his driving. He knew the main road like the back of his hand and Five Ways was a road junction about a quarter of the way from Warwick to Birmingham. The west fork of the junction went down to Rowington and then to places like Shrewley and Lapworth, along the Grand Union Canal, but off these secondary roads were lanes and byways that were known only to locals and the police.

The Range Rover was unfamiliar after his old car, but he liked it well enough and, even in tonight's bad conditions, he found it a pleasure to drive. The suburbs and villages slipped by in the October darkness. The roofs and pavements glistened in the wet and upstairs windows glowed redly as people went about their settling for the night.

He had passed Hatton and was now in the open stretch to Five Ways. The wipers beat like twin metronomes in front of his eyes and he compared the awful weather of the Midlands autumn with that of the Canary Islands and the Caribbean, where he had spent the last eight weeks, working hard to bury his horror in a languid round of shipboard socialising.

Had it worked? He didn't really know himself. Perhaps it had done something, but maybe it was just the passage of two months that had rubbed off the sharp edges of his grief. Maybe he could have saved himself a thousand pounds and stayed in Warwick with the same result. Feeling himself slipping into the familiar cycle of self-pity and recrimination, he savagely concentrated on his driving. He was almost glad that he had caught up with a large truck that half-filled the road. It gave him something to do, trying to pass it on the wet and slippery road.

When he finally pulled past it on a straight stretch, he found Five Ways right ahead of him. He imagined the truck driver cursing 'the silly buggers who overtake, then turn off!' But he had no choice and switched his indicators for a left turn.

The police car was parked a few yards down the side road. It was a white Jaguar with a red fluorescent band

6

around it and a blue flasher on the roof, which revolved to throw an eerie beam through the rain-filled air.

John Hardy pulled up right behind the Jaguar and flashed his headlights once to confirm who he was. The police driver stuck an arm out into the rain to give a 'thumbs up' sign and started to move away.

The Rover followed it for some miles down the side road, then turned left down an even smaller road for another mile. They were in raw agricultural country now, but patches of rough woodland began to appear wetly on either side of the lane. There seemed to be no more houses or cottages this way and Hardy saw only the gates of fields or gaping holes in hedges as his lights swept past.

The police car kept going, its bright red tail lights his only beacon in the pitch blackness. Then the right-hand flasher began winking its yellow message.

The sleek police vehicle turned slowly into what seemed to be a hole in the trees and Hardy saw that they were leaving the tarred road to go onto a gravel track. A few hundred yards in second gear and then he knew that they had arrived.

The Jaguar pulled up at the side of the lane, which here widened into a small clearing. There were other vehicles there, another white Jaguar, two Morris Eleven Hundreds and a Range Rover, all in police livery.

Beyond them were four more civilian cars, which Hardy guessed belonged to the senior detectives, photographers and maybe someone from the Home Office forensic laboratory.

Another car – a Mini – was parked opposite where he stopped and he saw a uniformed policeman stooping down to the driver's window. As he got out, he could just see a label on the windscreen saying 'Press'. Once again, he marvelled at the instinct that brought reporters to the scene of a crime, like a missile homing in by radar. If a body was found in the middle of the Gobi Desert, thought Hardy, he would not be surprised in the slightest if a spotty youth from the 'Wolverhampton Observer' popped up from behind the nearest boulder.

He took his case from the back and in the dim red light of the rear lamps, hopped on each foot to put on his gumboots. By now, shadowy figures were coming across from the other cars.

'Morning, Doc. Nice to see you back with us.'

The leader of the group of police officers was the man who had telephoned, Detective Chief Superintendent Lewis Carrol – inevitably known to the Force as 'Alice', though he certainly lived in no Wonderland. He was a squat figure in the dark, his breadth making his six-foot frame look shorter. He was pyramid-shaped, expanding progressively as one's eye went down from his small, bald head, past his shoulders to his broadening waist and massive legs and feet. Hardy had once seen him in swimming trunks and was reminded of a Japanese wrestler. But he was one hell of a good detective and was as tough as they come.

Behind him was Sam Partridge, Carrol's superintendent and the second man at Headquarters CID. Two others were shadows in the dark and Hardy gave them all a general greeting.

'Sorry to pull you out on a night like this, Doc,' Alice went on. 'But it's easing off a bit now.'

True enough, the heavy rain had almost stopped for the moment, though the overhanging trees still sent down a barrage of drips on them.

'We're down the lane a bit. I'll tell you as we go.'

Hardy walked alongside Carrol, the others following behind. They passed a knot of uniformed policemen standing by the cars, one talking through the window into a radio. The steady 'peep-peep' of the UHF set and the distorted jumble of number codes that came from the speaker, were suddenly so familiar to Hardy – and somehow soothing. The things that one knows and understands can be like a life-raft suddenly grabbed in a shipwreck, he thought – then sternly rejected it as being selfish nonsense.

The senior detective was talking as they passed the cars and headed down the muddy lane.

'It's far too mucky to bring the cars down here. And we didn't want to spoil any tracks more than we can help. Not that this damn rain is going to help – it'll already have washed out any tyre prints.'

'You said a girl, on the phone?'

'About twenty, maybe twenty-two, I should think. Hasn't been there long. Looks fresh to me, within the last day or two. Can't see any marks on her, but we haven't touched her yet, not until you have a look.'

Hardy plodded on, feeling his feet getting colder and damper in the disused rubber boots. They were walking on the dying autumn grass at the edge of the track, so as not to disturb any wheel marks that may have survived the rain.

'When was she found?'

'About nine o'clock. Sheer chance, really.'

Hardy stopped in the middle of the rough grass verge. 'Nine o'clock. In the pitch dark?'

Carrol grinned in the dark, so wide that Hardy could see his false teeth flashing in his little, wrinkled face.

'Yes, a farmer down the road lost one of his cows. Been looking for it since milking time. Still is, for all I know. Gate was left open and half a dozen of 'em wandered off. He found them all except one, doing his nut trying to round up the last one all evening. He came up through this little wood here, to see if it had fallen into an old quarry, where he's lost animals before.'

They began trudging on again.

'He didn't find a cow, but he found a girl. Took him a time to get the local officers down here to have a look.

Then they called us, so it was gone eleven before I got here. That's why we were so late in calling you, I'm afraid.'

Hardy's feet were distinctly wet now. Some of the long undergrowth had been spraying its moisture over the tops of his boots.

'Any idea who she is?'

Alice shook his head in the darkness. 'Not a clue yet. No handbag. We can't start a search until first light, for fear of messing up any tracks. Maybe something in her pockets, but we'll leave that until you get at it.'

The path had got muddier and more slippery and the rain began again, though not so heavy as before. Hardy saw torches flashing ahead, with a bigger, stronger light well amongst the trees to his left.

'Here we are, down this track. We're trying to keep away from the obvious route.'

A police constable stood at the side of the path, huddled in his mac. He held a clipboard, inadequately protected by the corner of a police cape that he had thrown over his raincoat. He stiffened and saluted as the chief superintendent came up to him.

'OK, son. Add Dr John Hardy, pathologist, to your list,' said Carrol and dived off left into the trees.

Hardy plunged after him, into longer weeds and sodden grass. There was enough soaking undergrowth here to make him wish that he had brought his fishing waders, not wellingtons.

Two lines of white plastic tape had been roughly lashed to saplings and bushes, to mark off a path into the wood. It confined the destructive effect of policemen's large feet to one passageway, to avoid trampling the whole area until it could be searched. Twenty yards down this track, he saw torches flitting about like fireflies.

'I'll go ahead, Doc. Watch your feet or you'll be over the edge. It's all overgrown, but there's a drop of about fifteen feet somewhere here.'

Sam Partridge, who was as tall and thin as his chief was squat, went ahead, his large rubber torch waving back and forth across the sodden ground.

The path dipped abruptly and Hardy slithered down, grabbing branches with his free hand, his bag knocking against trunks and saplings as he went.

Behind him, the chief superintendent plunged along, swearing as he missed his footing. Eventually, they slithered to a stop at a group of men, huddled round a tripod on which was a large lamp, connected by a tube to a cylinder of Calor gas. The hissing white light shone across into a green jungle, filling a large gouge in the steep bank down which they had just descended.

'She's in there, Doc,' said Carrol, pointing back to the further end of a wild overgrowth of nettles and brambles that filled the semicircle of a small quarry. Trees ringed the margin of the hole above them and the gas lamp cast an eerie glow halfway up their trunks.

John Hardy carefully set down his bag and looked at the scene. This was where mistakes began, if one wasn't careful. A boot on the wrong spot and a vital cigarette end might be crushed or a footprint obliterated.

He stood taking in the scene, his eyes roving around to orientate the position of the various landmarks. Behind him, Sam Partridge watched Hardy, knowing from experience that he wouldn't be rushed. He had worked with him on scores of such scenes and knew him for a pedantic, sometimes irritatingly careful worker, but one who could be utterly relied upon to give the best answer available.

From where Partridge stood, John Hardy was silhouetted against the lamplit background. Sam saw his neat, rather compact figure standing motionless and remembered other places, other times. He knew what Hardy had gone through recently, even though he hadn't been directly involved himself. Hardy's wife Jo, a general practitioner in Warwick, had volunteered to go into a house which was under siege by armed police. A mentally deranged man had kidnapped a boy and when the lad had developed pneumonia, Jo had insisted on trying to help him. She had been shot by the man when the police rushed the house and had later died in hospital. He wondered how a fifty-five-year-old doctor would adjust to the tragic loss of a younger, attractive wife. Would he rush off and get married to some dolly on the rebound – or would he stay as an ageing widower, getting more bitter and crotchety as the years went by? If he was any judge of a man, it wouldn't be the first way – though he could well imagine Hardy becoming more and more withdrawn, in his courteous, civilised way. His musing was interrupted by the motionless figure suddenly turning to Carrol.

'Which is the best way in, Mr Carrol?'

Alice pointed straight along the nearest side of the dip, between the profuse undergrowth and the black rock of the exposed side of the quarry.

'The floor of the quarry is almost level with where we are now, Doc ... except right at the back, where it dips down a few feet. The rear wall drops down sheer there, from those trees. That's where she was thrown in, by the looks of it.' Sam Partridge moved forward. 'All our approaches so far have been along this right-hand side. I don't think chummy – if there is a chummy – would have come down here. All the vegetation was standing intact when the first bobby got here.'

Hardy picked up his case again and gingerly followed Alice, who was moving forward into the dip.

Brambles tugged at his jacket and his feet squished ever deeper into what felt like a mixture of mud and cow dung. How often had he done this sort of thing in the middle of the night, he wondered? Then, almost suddenly, he saw her.

The object for which thirty men were standing about in the rain and for which by morning, maybe a hundred more would be involved. No trouble too much, no expense spared – that was the attitude of the police when the sinister word 'murder' was confirmed. And it was his job – and his alone – to confirm it.

'All yours, Doc,' muttered Carrol and stood aside.

Hardy slid past him in the narrow space between the rock face and the savage briars. The light from the gas lamp was shadowed here by the high undergrowth in the middle of the quarry, so the detective passed him a square hand-lamp.

Its yellow glow passed over the green and brown tangle of scrub, overshot on to the dripping black rock, then swung quickly back to fix on a crumpled shape lying on the dead brambles at the foot of the quarry wall.

She was lying almost on her face, her left arm outflung, her knees drawn up. For a moment, it seemed as if she were only sleeping. For all the hundreds of similar sights that Hardy had seen, he felt again the familiar twinge of sorrow for a young life so tragically ended. He knew only too well that it did not pay to be too outgoing with one's emotions in this job. A man has only a certain fund of compassion and to drain it too freely on each occasion would be asking too much of anyone. But now – especially now – he mourned for her. Very briefly, for there was work to be done.

He put his bag down behind him. Scanning the ground carefully in front of his feet, he moved forward warily until he could crouch at her side.

He called back over his shoulder at Lewis Carrol.

'What about photographs?'

'We've got them, from where you are now. I don't think there's anything to worry about on the ground. She must have been pitched down from up there.'

He jerked his head at the rock face.

'What about forensic – are they coming out?' asked Hardy, still not touching the body until he had double-checked that all the routine machinery of the investigation was functioning in the correct sequence.

'They're on their way. Should have got here the same time as you.'

Hardy looked back at the body. The girl's skin was dead white in the beam from his lamp. It looked all the more ghastly now, by contrast with the black dress she wore, a silky thing that was now sodden and stained with earth and lichen from the rock above.

The short skirt was rumpled up to her thighs and one shoulder of the garment seemed to be pulled down on to the upper arm. Her bedraggled blonde hair was tangled into the briars and the outflung hand was pulled into a little claw by rigor mortis.

'No harm in me getting right round her, is there?' called Hardy, without looking round.

'Carry on as you like, Doc. There won't be anything on the ground here from chummy. He must have stayed up top.'

The senior detective was assuming that the girl had been thrown into the dip from above – and Hardy, who rarely assumed anything, had to agree that it seemed highly unlikely that even a potential suicide would have jumped only fifteen feet into a mattress of brambles.

He spent a full minute looking at the position of the girl relative to her surroundings. Even the best photographs could never replace the first impressions of the scene, which could never be accurately reconstructed after the body had been moved.

His eyes took it all in and the intuitive processes began in his brain – comparing it with similar scenes with other bodies in similar surroundings. He was 'getting the feel of it' – something he could never adequately explain in cold black and white terms to students or other doctors.

The detectives waited patiently while Hardy's eyes took their fill. They knew that he was a damned good man to have at a time like this and they didn't try to chivvy him or hurry him up.

When he had seen enough, he humped himself nearer to the body, until he could touch it.

The back of the neck and the left side of the face were visible and he stretched out a hand to feel the skin. It was cold and wet, the clammy, rubbery feel of corpse flesh.

He gently took the outflung arm and moved it to see how stiff it was. The arm was rigid and the whole body tried to move when he levered gently against it.

'She's been dead since yesterday, at least. Not more than about two days,' he called over his shoulder. 'Best guess so far is the night before last – you know, Saturday night.'

It was now about one on Monday morning.

'Sure, Doc. We had the same sort of idea ourselves. Will you be able to get closer to a time than that?'

Hardy permitted himself a half-smile in the darkness. The first two questions the police always had were 'Who is it?' and 'How long has she been dead?'

'Not too hopeful. You know what I think of estimating time of death. But we'll see when we get her out.'

Now he moved her head slightly more to the left, pulling against the death stiffness. The neck was rigid, but he managed to get a better view of her face. There were scratches on the cheeks from briars, but no other marks, except for the blotchy discoloration of the dead. The eyes were wide open and he gently pulled down one lower lid with his thumb. There was nothing abnormal to be seen. The first tingles of anxiety began to crawl up the back of his neck. Not strangled – he could see the neck easily, as the black dress was low-cut. No bleeding, no knife or bullet wounds on the parts exposed. No signs of asphyxia in the eyes or skin.

Still, it was early days yet.

'Nothing to be seen so far, Mr Carrol,' he called back.

'Right, Doc. I think forensic have arrived. Can you hang on a tick before you do any more?'

Hardy squatted back on his heels, relaxing. He was keeping a corpse close company again, a job he had done times without number. Behind him, there was some crashing and cursing and a brighter light approached.

The newcomer had a big electric hand-lantern which cast enough light upwards to show a wild shock of hair and thick glasses.

'Morning, John. What have we got?'

Hardy looked up from his crouching position. The tops of his gumboots were cutting into the backs of his knees and the muscles of his thighs were beginning to ache.

'Hello, Archie. How are you?'

Neither found anything incongruous in these civilised greetings at such a place, at such a time.

'Fine, fine. Nice to have you back, haven't seen you in ages.'

The niceties over, Hardy returned to the business in hand.

'Girl about twenty, thrown down from the edge of the quarry, by the looks of it. No obvious cause of death, so far.'

Archie Salmon was a scientist from the Home Office Forensic Science laboratory. A graduate biologist, he affected a 'mad professor' look, but his experience and shrewdness matched that of Hardy, in his own field of expertise.

He shuffled up to squat alongside Hardy and, like the doctor, stopped to take a long, hard look. Neither spoke for a long time.

'Not much point in trying to do much here,' said Archie finally. Hardy grunted in agreement. A shudder born of cold and damp suddenly racked him from head to foot.

'I'm getting too old for these wet nights, Archie.' He slowly ran his torch up and down the length of the still body. 'I agree, there's little we can do here. We'll have to get her out first.'

The scientist was using his own more powerful lamp and the beam rested on the outstretched arm of the girl.

'What's that mark – the one on the wrist?'

Hardy squinted along the path of the lamp.

'Something there. Looks rather like the mark made by a watch strap or a bracelet.'

His own lamp had not been strong enough to show it up before. They both looked at it for a moment, then Hardy rose to his feet, grimacing at the cramp in his legs.

'Let's get her out, then. All the pictures have been taken, according to Mr Carrol.'

He was always very correct in mentioning the names of others, right down to the last police constable. But Archie had no such inhibitions.

'Alice!' he yelled, 'Any objections to us getting on with it?' He had known the chief superintendent since the latter was a sergeant and had no compunction about using his nickname. It was all part of his carefully cultivated eccentricity.

Carrol edged along the quarry face towards them.

'Sure, do what you like. We're stuck until we get the scene clear. We couldn't rig up the plastic tent to keep the rain off, because of all these bloody brambles.'

Archie Salmon yelled again, this time over Alice's head, at a shadowy figure standing with the other detectives at the lower edge of the quarry.

'Ted, bring up that big polythene sheet, will you?'

A moment later, the liaison officer from the forensic laboratory passed a folded sheet along the track, until it reached Hardy. He partly unfolded it and laid it carefully along the back of the body. Then, with Archie Salmon and

Lewis Carrol holding both lamps to light up the corpse, he gently rolled the girl over, so that she lay partly on the plastic sheet.

Now he could see the side hidden from him until then.

The underside of the face and neck was stained purplish – red due to the settling of the blood in the tissues. The stiff left arm now stuck up towards him and the bent legs balanced precariously on the heels. He held the body with one hand while he looked at the crushed vegetation where she had been lying.

There seemed to be nothing unusual to be seen.

'Hang on, Doc, I'll pull the sheet through.'

The biologist pulled the polythene under the body, much as a nurse puts a draw-sheet under a patient in a hospital bed.

'OK, you can let her go now.'

Hardy released the arm of the girl and she rolled over on to the opposite side, now completely on the plastic. Anything that fell off the body in transit to the mortuary, would now be trapped on the transparent material and could be recovered for examination.

'I'll have to break the rigor in the arm, or we'll never get her into any transport,' murmured Hardy. He gently pressed on the outstretched arm until he felt the rigid muscles give way.

'Mr Carrol, I think she must have been here for almost all the time since she died,' he said over his shoulder.

'How d'you tell that, Doc?''

'The settling of the blood – the post-mortem lividity – is all on the lowest side. She must have been dumped here within a few hours of death.'

He carefully wrapped the wide expanse of spare polythene over the pathetic figure and parcelled the whole body into a neat package.

'What about transport?' asked Archie.

'We've got no undertaker out, I'm afraid,' answered

Carrol. 'There's a stretcher-type carrier in the Special Incident Range Rover. Will that do you?'

Hardy weighed up the marginal advantages of waiting for a light fibreglass 'shell' coffin to be brought from town, against the prospect of standing guard over the corpse in the cold and wet for at least another hour.

The numbness of his toes won the day.

'We'll take her out now. I can't see any advantage in waiting, can you, Archie?'

The forensic scientist shook his shaggy head.

'Let's get on with the show,' he said.

Chapter Two

Lewis Carrol looked a little peeved. He sat in a rickety easy chair in the tiny office of the hospital mortuary, his damp mackintosh reaching the floor, framing his massive feet in their great boots.

The mouth below his bulbous nose was turned down and he looked distinctly sour.

'The point is, Doc – have we or have we not got a murder on our hands?'

Hardy stood at a washbasin in the corner, lathering his hands. He still wore a green gown and a pair of white rubber boots. As he slowly slid the soapsuds around his fingers, he decided on an answer for the chief superintendent.

'I don't know,' he said finally. 'From the surrounding circumstances, it's hard to see what else it could be.'

Alice's lumpy face looked even more unhappy.

'That's a hell of an answer,' he grunted.

Across the room, Sam Partridge and Archie Salmon watched points. They sensed an impending bit of friction between the two main characters.

John Hardy finished his washing and began rubbing himself up to the elbows with a threadbare hospital towel.

'I'm not trying to be difficult, Mr Carrol,' he began quietly, 'but you must appreciate my point of view. It's not the slightest use my giving you a string of half-truths that would be cut to pieces the minute the case got inside any court of law.'

The detective clasped his hands in his lap, the fingers like two interlocking bunches of bananas. 'Sure, Doc. But what did she die from, for crying out loud?'

Hardy sank onto a hard chair near the battered desk and wearily kicked off the boots, groping for his own shoes with one hand.

'We'll have to go through the whole thing, stage by stage, and see what the options are,' he suggested.

Alice snorted. 'Beg your pardon, Doc, but sod the options! I've got to pick up that phone in a minute and ring the Chief. What the hell am I to tell him?'

Hardy sighed, but silently. He didn't feel up to arguing with a bloody-minded detective at three thirty in the morning.

'If you want the simple answer, we've got to treat it as a case of homicide until proved otherwise. And I say homicide, not murder, because it could be manslaughter. And, of course, it could even turn out to be an accident.'

'What about suicide?' asked Partridge. He wasn't trying to be funny.

Hardy shook his head. 'That's about the one thing it isn't. It might be anything else – even natural causes. But not suicide.'

Lewis Carrol groaned. 'Jesus, Doc, where did you go on that holiday? You used to snap us out the answer right on the nail before.'

Hardy felt the first twinge of real annoyance, but he tried to cover it over with a patch of humour.

'I didn't get sunstroke, if that's what you mean. This case is a stinker. I didn't choose it, you know.'

There was a temporary lull in the proceedings as the mortuary attendant brought in a tin tray with half a dozen cups of tea. He had brewed up on the window sill of the refrigerator room, where he had an electric kettle and an assortment of odd cups, some with handles.

He was a small man with hair like frayed yellow rope. His face was permanently set in an expression of surprise, but he was a cheerful, efficient little man, even when

22

hauled out of bed in the middle of the night to do 'a special', as he called it.

They all took a cup and Hardy received a blue mug with a great crack down one side. He drank from it with mild distaste but curbed his fastidious urge to refuse it for fear of hurting the attendant's feelings.

'Come on then, Doc. Give us the options,' said Alice, ladling sugar into his cup from a paper packet on the table.

Hardy set his mug on the table and folded his arms over his gown.

'Let's look at the facts. We've got a girl – so far unidentified, about twenty years old. Died probably the night before last, that's say between twenty-four and thirty-six hours ago. She's been raped, or if not actual rape, there's been some overenthusiastic intercourse, to say the least.'

Archie Salmon blinked through his thick lenses.

'No panties on, bruises and scratches between the thighs.'

Sam Partridge pushed himself off the wall he'd been leaning against. 'A lot of dollies don't wear pants, especially when they're expecting a bit of action.'

Partridge had a laconic sense of humour, which never deserted him. Hardy sipped his tea gingerly.

'They either weren't worn or they've been dumped. She had no tights on either. I'd have thought that odd, in this weather. But that's not part of the medical angle. The next thing is that her wrists have been tied together and that was done before death.'

'How do you know that, Doc,' asked Carrol.

'Little pinhead haemorrhages along the line of the cord – and some bruising in the tissues underneath. Whatever was around her wrists must have been pulled pretty tight.'

The man from the forensic laboratory put his pennyworth in here.

'It was so tight that the pattern of the rope was imprinted into the skin. A spiral about a centimetre wide.' Archie had gone totally metric, much to the exasperation of certain Crown Court judges, who insisted that he converted them into inches by agile mental arithmetic in the witness box.

Hardy nodded. 'A narrow rope or even the cord of a dressing gown.'

'Telephone wire … pyjama cord?' hazarded Partridge.

'No … they're plaited, not spiral,' countered Salmon.

Hardy took another sip at his tea, trying to conceal his distaste for the almost black liquid.

'Next point – the girl has no injuries apart from the minor ones associated with forceful sex. Nothing to kill her, anyway. Nor is there any sign of natural disease to the naked eye.'

'So she shouldn't be dead, Doc. But she is,' challenged Lewis Carrol.

Archie Salmon came in to back up Hardy.

'We've got a long way to go investigation-wise yet. Drugs, alcohol, poisons.'

Hardy completed the list, 'Microscopic examination for rare types of heart disease. Though that's a bit of a thin hope.'

'And, if they all turn out negative?'

'Let's wait and see, shall we?'

Hardy's voice was mild. He thought it better not to express the sixth sense that told him that this case was going to be the frustrating one that turns up once a year and defies all efforts to crack.

'There are other causes of death, which the pathologist cannot be expected to confirm just on the results of a post-mortem,' he added. 'People tend to think that the mortuary slab is the absolute answer every time. I'm afraid that just isn't so.'

The chief superintendent scowled at him, deep wrinkles

appearing on his forehead and travelling up onto the bald wasteland above.

'You're talking yourself out of a job, Doc.'

Hardy allowed himself a polite smile.

'You've seen them yourself, Mr Carrol. With me, over the years. A jab in the neck, like the old commando punch – stops the heart and sometimes not a thing to show for it. Suffocation ... usually leaves signs, I admit, but sometimes it doesn't. Sheer fright can kill – falling into cold water, the criminal abortion. The old word was "vagal inhibition". Didn't mean a thing, but what's in a name?'

Alice stood up, gathering his voluminous riding mac around him. 'I've got to ring the Old Man. Standing orders with a suspicious death. We've got a probable rape, and a definite tying-up, and a concealment of the body. And she's dead, so that's good enough to be going on with. I hope to God you boffins can dig up something more definite pretty soon.'

'We'll be in touch, Super,' said Archie touching his shaggy forelock as the detectives marched out to their car radio.

Hardy shrugged off his gown and reached for his jacket. 'Do your best for me, Archie. Find something or our friend will burst a blood vessel.'

It was half past four by the time Hardy put the Rover back into the garage. Instead of going to bed in the lonely house, he walked slowly into his study and sank down into his favourite armchair. Since coming back from his cruise, he had hardly been in the room and he sat for a time staring around, soaking up the familiar things. The certificates and diplomas on the walls, commendations from a variety of international organisations. Pictures of university cricket teams, even one of his old prep school; a narrow strip of a hundred scrubbed faces staring out on to a pre-war world.

He looked at his ranks of books standing against the

walls, almost every forensic book that had been published in the last thirty years, some in German and French.

In a corner was a small desk where a secretary had used the typewriter, now shrouded and silent under its grey cover. And on his own big, beautiful desk – the picture of Jo, smiling and serene. Her stethoscope still hung on the back of the door, but it would never be used again.

The room was cold; the radiator had been off since last spring. He felt icy himself, but he hadn't the will to get up and go back to bed.

The events of the night had pushed him further back into his apathy. Not because it had been a dead woman, as Jo was a dead woman. But because the indeterminate result, the unanswered questions, all crowded in on him. He felt unequal to fighting back as he always had done, fighting back with relish.

He had felt the implied criticisms of the detectives, who were used to getting a straight answer on the spot. But he was a doctor, not a soothsayer. He gave them the range of possibilities; they had no right to expect an answer based on extrasensory perception, which is what it would have been if he had picked some answers from the air to satisfy them.

Angrily, a sudden burst of spirit pushed him up out of the chair. Things had come to a pretty state if he was reduced to moaning to himself about his staunch friends, the police. They had their job to do and a damned difficult, thankless one it was. It was up to him to give them all the help he could and where his help ran dry, to at least be patient with them and suggest the next moves.

He strode out of the room, turned off the light and marched across to the kitchen to make himself some coffee and toast.

Yet as he sat at the kitchen table, the brief moment of defiance gradually melted away and he found himself acutely aware of being alone. The kitchen was too big without Jo. The whole house was too big and too empty without her. He felt adrift, aimlessly wandering down a broad road of pointless, mundane daily activities.

The thought of another ten or so years of this life until he retired was suddenly an abomination to Hardy. He looked around the neat kitchen as if he was seeing it for the first time. What in God's name did he want all this for? He had no intention of getting married again or even taking a mistress. He felt drained and aimless, like a rudderless ship on a still sea.

The few months that had gone by since Jo had languished in hospital after the shooting were an unreal interlude, not related to what went before or after. Hardy recognised now that he had merely been escaping from himself and his circumstances, diverting his mind by petty excursions and trivial occupations. Now he was back and he was exactly where he was the day that Jo died. He had delayed the confrontation with himself, but not sidestepped it or even blunted the sharpness of the problem. And the problem was, what was he to do with the rest of – his life?

The urge to start from scratch somewhere else was strong upon him. He wanted to shake off the constraints of this town and all its associations, however happy they had been at the time. He felt uneasy in his office and in the University generally. People he had known for years suddenly seemed strangers again, only because they felt awkward when they came up to offer their condolences. It raised a barrier that would take a long time to lower and he didn't feel up to making the effort to speed up the process. Far better to start again afresh, a long way off.

The cup was empty, the plate had just a few crumbs. He looked at the clock and saw that it was still only five o'clock.

With a sigh, he hauled himself up from the chair and went to bed. He felt old and alone. The realisation was far from pleasant.

The police had set up their murder room in the Divisional Station in Norton Heath, between the scene of the incident and Birmingham. It was the nearest town and, as they had no identity yet for the girl, the chief superintendent decided that one place was as good as another.

The red brick police station was a solid-looking building of late nineteen thirties vintage. It stood near the civic centre of the town, which was now almost an industrial suburb of Birmingham, barely five miles of market gardens and small factories separating it from the sprawl of the huge conurbation to the north.

Norton Heath had mushroomed since the war and was moving fast along the main road to meet its giant neighbour. It had several motor component factories which fed the huge assembly plants at Longbridge and Coventry. The advent of a huge outstation of a Government department fleeing from London had given it another transfusion of people and affluence. The little market town of the turn of the century was now a mini-Detroit, complete with super-supermarkets, ice rink and two nightclubs.

It was to one of these clubs that the patient work of the murder room led Lewis Carrol on the second day after the discovery of the body.

No distraught mother had come forward to report the disappearance of her daughter and Alice had settled down resignedly to a long search. The photographs taken at the post-mortem had provided a picture of the girl's face and after some judicious touching-up of the discoloration, they were being printed for widespread distribution.

The teeth were in perfect condition and there seemed little point in starting a full-blown enquiry amongst dentists, with so little to go on.

'Damn all, that's what we've got,' he muttered to Sam

Partridge, as he stood at the door of the recreation room in the Norton Heath station. The table tennis had been packed away and trestles set up around the room. The inevitable blackboard was there, with a new box of chalk, but so far no one had found anything to draw. Half a dozen detective constables sat at the tables, fiddling with a few pieces of paper and one man was on a telephone, taking a call from a member of the public.

'Looks like Wigan in the General Strike,' grunted Sam. 'All dressed up and nowhere to go. Bloody fine murder this is ... if it is a murder?'

Carrol sat his broad backside on the middle of an empty trestle table. 'She didn't chuck herself down that quarry, Sam. She was dead before she got there, according to John Hardy. Something to do with cuts from those brambles not bleeding.'

Partridge thought for a minute. 'He still hasn't come up with what killed her? If we get a villain, what do we charge him with?'

'Causing death by fright, perhaps,' answered his chief, with some sarcasm.

The plain-clothes constable who had been on the telephone came across rather diffidently, a sheet of paper in his hand.

'Excuse me, sir. I don't know if this is anything worth following up.' He held out the paper and the chief superintendent took it with a frown. He read it, then handed it across to Sam Partridge.

'Know the girl who said this, lad?'

The detective shook his head. 'No, sir. But I know the Saracen, it's on our blacklist of clubs.'

Partridge gave the paper back to the younger man.

'I know the Saracen, all right. Whores' rendezvous – and a bit of drug passing and illegal gaming, we suspect.'

Alice thumped back onto the floor. 'Enter that in the books, lad. Worth checking out.' He looked across the room to where a tall thin man was searching through a tin of biscuits, trying to find a ginger nut.

'Oi, Davies! Come here!'

Davies, a detective sergeant, dropped the tin and hurried over.

'Davies, we've had a call from a girl who works as a hostess in some crummy club. You'll know it, the Saracen, down the road here. Her girlfriend, who shares a room with her, hasn't shown up for three nights. Nip out and bring her in, there's a good lad. Get the details from the feller filling the log over there.

Davies trotted off and the two senior detectives looked at each other.

'Get any twinges, Sam?' asked Carrol.

'She's twenty-one and missing the right length of time. It's the nearest town and she's likely to be on the game, at least part-time. All fits together, though maybe it's too easy to be true.'

'We don't deserve it, I'll admit. Not a stroke of work has anyone done yet. Waiting for those damn photos to be printed and for forensic to do their stuff.'

Partridge slapped a fist into his palm.

'Forensic … I forgot to tell you. They rang through a half-hour back, to say the girl had a positive result for seminal fluid inside her. And that she had a moderate amount of alcohol. Hundred and thirty milligrammes, they said.'

Carrol paced up and down the empty square in the middle of the room, between the faded lines marked out for badminton.

'I don't know Norton Heath all that well. What sort of club life they got here?'

'Two of 'em. One quite respectable, sort you could take your missus to on a charity night. No messing about, straight cabaret, bit of stripping on stag nights. But all above board.'

'And the other one?'

'That's this Saracen place. A pain in the bloody brain to the local super. Changed its name twice, lost its licence for a year. Looking fair to be shut down again.

'Rough, is it?'

'Not so much rough as wicked. Plenty of money put into the decorations and that. Like a Tangier brothel inside, all red lights and velvet curtains. But the riff-raff and the girls get in there. We've had a couple of knock-downs for cannabis. Picked up the girls a couple of times, but the manager's too damn smart to carry the can.'

'Who runs it then?'

'Feller called Dickie Durrant. Ex-con artist, done time for it, but he's stayed clean a long while now. But he doesn't own it.'

Alice waited, standing there in a crumpled Suit, letting the ash from his cigarette drop unheeded down his lapels.

'Monty Lever owns it,' said Partridge.

The chief superintendent's eyes swivelled round to meet Sam's.

'Monty Lever? That bugger?'

He started walking again.

'The plot thickens, Sam. We all know Monty, don't we. I'd love to hang one on him. Murder, preferably. Damn Hardy and his messing about.'

Sam looked after his boss, who was .pacing away from him, stumping across the floor on his wide-spread legs.

'Easy on, sir. We don't even know who the girl is yet, let alone if Monty is mixed up in anything.'

Alice pressed his lumpy nose with a thick finger.

'I smell it, Sam. I smell Lever in this. Something like this would be just his cup of tea.'

Partridge sent his mind back eleven years, to another Division on the other side of Birmingham. Monty Lever had been given seven years for rape but had the verdict quashed on appeal on some legal grounds, thanks to his high-powered lawyers.

Years before that, he had done two years in prison for assault. Apart from these, the police had a long score card of unproven villainies in which he might well have been involved.

But wishful thinking didn't cut any ice in a Crown Court.

'No use jumping to conclusions,' he said wistfully.

'Why not?' countered Carrol, with an evil grin. 'Makes me warm all over, just to think of putting the boot into Monty Lever. Come on, Davies, hurry back with that girl.'

Twenty minutes later, the dead girl was identified as Joyce Daniels. Her friend, the one that phoned the murder room, was a brassy young blonde, describing herself as a photographic model and part-time hostess at the Saracen Club. Her name was Sylvia Marsh and she seemed genuinely worried that something might have happened to her room-mate.

'Never gone off this long before,' she said to Sam Partridge, as she sat on a hard chair in the middle of the badminton court, ringed by three detectives. 'She might have gone off for a night with a feller, but not three nights on the trot. Not without coming back and telling me, anyway.'

Alice jerked his head at Davies and the thin constable produced a copy of the photo that had been touched-up for the posters.

'Was this her, love?'

The hardbitten club hostess, who would have stolen the last halfpenny from a client, surprisingly burst into a torrent of tears. The coal-black make-up around her narrow eyes ran down her face as she sniffed and snuffled into a grubby tissue that she dragged from her handbag.

'That's her, is it?' prompted Partridge gently.

Sylvia sniffed and nodded. 'It's a rotten picture, but

that's Joyce all right,' she snivelled.

'When did you see her last?'

'Friday night. In the club. She was there till about eleven.'

Partridge looked at Lewis Carrol.

'Tuesday morning now. That fits for time.'

He bent over the girl again, who was rubbing at her smeared eyes with the tissue.

'You'll have to come down with us, love, and have a quick look at the body. We've got to be sure about it.'

Numbly, the blonde let herself be led by Partridge towards the door.

'Go with him, Davies. I'll hold the fort here.'

The chief superintendent rubbed his hands together in anticipation.

'Ring me from the mortuary to confirm the identification, Sam. Then we can stop all these damn posters going out and get cracking on some real action.'

After they had left, he got a police cadet to make him a cup of Nescafé and then sat down to dream about hanging a murder charge on Monty Lever, his Private Enemy Number One.

'Look, Doc, can you get any nearer at all to a time of death for us.'

There was pleading in Carrol's voice as he asked Hardy the same question again. He was in Hardy's room at the University, late the same afternoon. Sam Partridge leaned against the wall near the door and Evan Williams, the Norton Heath divisional detective inspector was perched on a stool in the corner. John Hardy sat behind his desk, where he had been signing routine post-mortem reports when the detectives descended on him. His office was tucked away on the third floor of the Faculty of Medicine building in the University. Hardy was glad that he spent only part of his time there, as it had no windows at all and was jammed in between a noisy lift shaft and a chemical laboratory which seemed to have whining centrifuges going for most of the day. The office was only about twelve feet square and half the volume was occupied by green filing cabinets.

At the moment, most of the other half was filled with these large policemen.

Alice was parked on a chair in front of him, directly across the other side of the desk. Partridge thought they looked like a pair of cockerels squaring up for a fight. But there was no animosity between them, only an intense desire to get to the bottom of the whole affair.

'There's honestly no more that I can give you in that direction,' Hardy was saying, calmly but firmly. 'I saw the body at about one o'clock in the morning. Her temperature was down exactly to that of the surrounding air. She was a slim girl, hardly any clothes on worth talking about, apart from a bra and that silly dress, so she would have cooled very quickly in that chilly, wet weather.'

He paused, but Carrol made no reply, just kept staring intently into his face, so he went on.

'There was full rigor mortis, for what that's worth. Taking it all into account, I guess at between twenty and thirty hours since death, though even that could be wrong by a good margin.'

'Wrong which way, Doc?' put in Partridge.

'Impossible to say,' answered Hardy.

Carrol grunted. 'And that's the nearest you can get?'

John Hardy tried to conceal his irritation, which seemed to be nearer the surface than usual, these days.

'I could say anything you'd like to hear and still be justified by some people's standards,' he replied, rather tartly. 'But what's the use of that, when counsel at the trial could tear it apart in three minutes and use it to denigrate the rest of my evidence?'

'I thought there were fancy new tests these days,'

persisted Carrol. 'With blood and other fluids – you know, chemical tests.'

Hardy made a deprecating gesture with his hand.

'Quite unreliable, I'm afraid. I used to play about with them, but they're not much use at all. As a famous pathologist used to say, the only way to tell the time of death accurately is to be there when it happens.'

'You're destroying my faith in science, Doc,' grumbled Alice.

Hardy laughed, a humourless bark.

'You've been reading the sort of detective novels where a police surgeon lays a hand on the forehead of the corpse and says he died at twenty past three last Tuesday week. I'm afraid that sort of thing fell into disrepute years ago.'

The chief superintendent hauled himself to his feet. 'So we haven't got a cause of death and we don't know the time of death?' he said heavily, with a tone that hardly concealed his lack of pleasure.

John Hardy stood up as well and the two stocky men faced each other across the desk.

'I've given you the best time of death that any honest pathologist could offer you, Mr Carrol. Is it that vital? Are you trying to break an alibi?'

Carrol shrugged. 'As it happens, it doesn't matter all that much, but it would have been nice to have a set time to fling in Lever's face. He's got his usual put-up alibi, organised from amongst his cronies and employees in the clubs. But without any better evidence we're not going to get around to testing it.'

'He denies all knowledge of the girl, presumably.'

The conversation was rubbing away the bristly patch that had formed between the two men.

'Admits he knew her – he could hardly do otherwise, as he employed the girl. But says he hadn't been near the Saracen that night or for the two previous nights. Says he has a manager to do the work for him, why should he keep a dog and bark himself? No one saw him out with the girl at any time and certainly not that night.'

Hardy nodded, rubbing his chin thoughtfully. 'No direct evidence from his car or something like that?'

Sam Partridge did the head shaking this time.

'We could get no tyre traces from that lane – the rain had washed everything out. And we've no opportunity to check out any of his cars, as we have nothing to bring a charge against him.'

'And she had no bleeding to leave stains in a car. The chances of finding hair or something are slim, but possible.

But without access to the car, we haven't got a hope.'

'And his solicitor is such hot stuff on his rights that we daren't try to wangle something with a traffic charge, just to get a look at the cars,' put in Partridge.

'Of which he's got about four – and umpteen more belonging to all his assistant villains,' concluded Carrol.

Hardy nodded sympathetically. 'I'm waiting for the microscope sections to see if I can raise some cause of death for you, but I'll admit that it's a slight chance. I'm sure in my own mind she died sometime on Saturday night, early Sunday morning, but if pressed hard in the witness box, I would have my work cut out even to justify that degree of accuracy.'

Hardy sounded regretful, but adamant that he would be pushed no further into speculation.

The detectives moved towards the door and the silent Inspector Williams opened it for them.

As the senior man went out, he paused and turned back to Hardy.

'The Press are getting a bit restive, as I can't tell them a thing. I suppose the coroner will open an inquest in the next day or two and when they hear there's no cause of death, they're likely to get sarcastic.'

Hardy refused to rise to the bait.

'I've spoken to the coroner about it already. He accepts what I told him, that I can't invent a cause of death, if I don't know one. If he doesn't like the way I do his post-mortems, he's perfectly entitled to get some other pathologist who can.'

Carrol gave one of his grunts and vanished. Sam paused long enough to give Hardy a large conspiratorial wink, then lumbered after him.

'The divisional detective inspector, whom Hardy knew better than any of the others, cleared his throat and spoke in a rather self-conscious way. 'Don't worry, Doc. It'll all come out in the wash.'

Hardy sat looking at the closed door when they had all gone. A kind of delayed annoyance crept over him.

What the devil am I supposed to be – a physician or a magician?

Chapter Three

Hardy got up next day in a mood of defiant determination. The black clouds that had been hovering over him were still there, but his very nature forced him to fight back.

He climbed out of bed, had a shower and shaved, then went downstairs to make his usual frugal breakfast of toast and coffee.

He tried to ignore the resounding silence in the house. Deliberately, he clashed the dirty dishes together when he left them in the sink for Mrs Townsend, his daily woman. He stamped his feet a little more aggressively than usual and turned on the transistor radio to an unnecessarily loud level as he went up to finish dressing.

As a final challenge to the world, he slammed the back door loudly and went to his car.

The three mile drive to the University provided no further opportunities for him to defy the gods, but once in his office, he decided to do twice as much work as possible that day.

He had an undergraduate lecture at nine o'clock and he spoke for an hour on 'Medical negligence and how to avoid it', without pausing to draw breath.

The attendance was rather poor and he fancied that the few stalwarts who had managed to climb out of bed to come to hear him were rather lacking in attentiveness. Perhaps it was his current paranoia over the Joyce Daniels affair, but he fancied that some of the students were whispering behind their hands a bit more than usual.

At ten o'clock, he strode into the mortuary and tore into the four routine post-mortem examinations, perhaps clashing the knives about a bit more loudly than usual.

He worked through until twenty to twelve, missing his morning coffee, then hurried back to his office to dictate the reports and some letters.

Still full of his new-found dynamism, he resurrected a half-written article that he had promised an American journal three months before and started to reread it, to get up 'flying speed' for its completion.

But at twelve-fifteen the phone rang. It was PC Herbert, the coroner's officer from Norton Heath.

'Sorry to give such short notice, Doctor Hardy,' said the fruity voice of the coroner's right-hand man, 'but Mr Kieller wants to open an inquest this afternoon on this Joyce Daniels.'

Hardy felt a sudden deflation, as this case again rose up in the forefront of his mind. 'What time?'

'Four fifteen, please, Doc. Won't take ten minutes, but they want to get rid of the body.'

The moment he replaced the phone, it rang again.

'Archie Salmon, John. Thought you might like a little bit of news.'

'What's that? Hope it's something good for a change.'

'So-so. That seminal swab we got from the post-mortem on the girl. It's a Group B and naturally, the chap is a secretor.'

Hardy was puzzled. This was not news worth a sixpenny phone call.

'What's the significance of that, Archie? We've no one to match it with.'

The forensic scientist's voice cackled over the line. His laugh matched his eccentric appearance.

'We have, you know! Remember that Monty Lever was done for rape, eleven years ago. I looked up our files and found that he's a B-secretor, too.'

Hardy considered this for a moment. Of the four blood groups, Group B was the third most common, being present only in about nine per cent of the British population. Furthermore, only about seventy percent of the population were 'secretors'. This meant that they had the blood group in their other body fluids, like saliva and semen, so the match was quite significant.

'Do the CID know yet?' he asked.

'Just rang them. All the big noises were out, but I've left a message.'

'Yes, they've only just gone from here. But Archie, don't be too full of rejoicing about this. They've got nothing to charge Lever with and, unless they do, they can't use that blood group evidence. And, of course, it's only an exclusory test. Even though a B is much better than an A or an O, there must still be a few million of them in Britain.'

Archie refused to be depressed. 'Sure, we know all about that, happens twice a day in this lab. But it's a hell of a sight better than finding that the groups were totally different, which would have put that slug Lever right in the clear.'

'I gather he's not one of your favourite people, Archie,' suggested Hardy.

'You can say that again. I was in the rape case, all those years ago. He was as guilty as Judas, but his smart lawyers got him off the hook. I'd love to see him done this time.'

After the call, Hardy saw that it was hopeless trying to do anything more to his paper and reluctantly put it back into its drawer.

He walked across to the Senior Common Room and had a pre-lunch sherry and looked at the newspapers. The local rags were plastered with the Joyce Daniels case, though they had no news and made do with puffing all the rumours into a nothing-type story. They had interviews with a synthetically tearful aunt in Stoke-on-Trent, who had brought the girl up after her parents had run in opposite directions when their marriage broke up years before. The girl had left school at the earliest opportunity, worked in a few shops, then vanished from the sight of her aunt, who hadn't seemed to have lifted a finger to find where Joyce had gone. There were pictures of the girl, her aunt, the girlfriend who identified her and of the lane and wood where the body was found. But of hard news there was not a scrap and some veiled complaints were included about the police being uncooperative in releasing any further information. A paragraph in slightly bolder type informed the readers that *Dr John Hardy, forensic pathologist from the University of Warwick, conducted a post-mortem examination, but so far the authorities have given no clue as to the way in which the girl died, a most unusual omission in the circumstances.*

He finished his Dry Fly and went into the high, airy staff dining room of the University. It was about half-full and he stood for a moment at the door, picking a place to sit.

'John, come and join me.'

A tall, silver-haired man waved to him from a nearby table. It was James Donnington, the Dean of the Medical Faculty, a senior pathologist, turned university administrator.

He was a friend of Hardy's, though the association was more one of parallel personalities and common medical interests, rather than any underlying personal warmth.

Donnington was the head of the medical part of Warwick University and to some extent was Hardy's 'boss', if such a thing could be said to exist in the peculiar government of a university.

'Sit down and tell me all the gory details. I read in the local rag that you've had some odd death again.'

Donnington was an intellectual snob and though he read the Warwick newspapers from front to back, he did this in private, preferring to be seen carrying the *Times* and *Telegraph* under his arm.

He was an academic pathologist – or had been until he had shed teaching and research for his present administrative position. He tended to look down on the practical, often unsavoury, job that Hardy did and usually referred to it in a bantering, derogatory way.

As they ate their way through lunch, John Hardy told him some of the details of the Joyce Daniels case. Strictly speaking, such matters were highly confidential, but between two pathologists the professional interest was similar to two surgeons discussing a patient.

Hardy had known Donnington for twenty years and knew that his discretion was absolute. There was also the factor that Donnington had been an excellent pathologist, albeit in a very specialist field and might have some useful advice on occasions. In fact, in this particular case, his opinion might be relevant.

'Sudden death of twenty-year-old and nothing at all to show for it,' mused Donnington. 'Plenty of possibilities, but few of them provable, eh?'

Hardy had reached his cheese and biscuits. He shrugged as he carefully slit a piece of double Gloucester in two. 'A sudden heart arrest might be the best explanation – the "vagal inhibition" that the old pathologists used to waffle about.'

Donnington frowned. 'Steady on, old chap. I'm an old pathologist and I was very fond of vagal inhibition. Used to cover a multitude of sins, years ago. Nice vague term.'

Hardy dropped his knife onto his plate in irritation.

'Can't afford to be vague these days. Queen's Counsel are too well up on medical matters. They'd nail you to the wall if you trotted out vagal inhibition, with nothing else to back it up.'

Donnington looked slightly offended. 'So what do you say, you modern chaps?'

I usually say I don t know. That's even more vague, but honest.'

The Dean of Medicine sniffed, to convey his disapproval. 'That doesn't help anyone, does it?'

'Doesn't harm anyone, either. No, James, the choices here seem to be between a cardiac arrest – a fancy new way of saying vagal inhibition, if you like – or some obscure heart condition, like a myocarditis. That's your field – or used to be.'

Donnington looked a little mollified. 'I did a bit of work on it, I'll admit. But you can look down a microscope as well as I can. Any joy in that direction?'

Hardy shook his head. 'Not had the blocks through yet. Should be through this afternoon. I've got the inquest at four-fifteen, so I'll have to look at the heart sections pretty smartly and then dash off to tell the coroner what I think.'

James Donnington shook his head sadly. 'Not the way to do pathology, John. Rushing about, snatching a glance here, a guess there.'

Hardy smiled bleakly. 'Try telling that to the police and the coroner. They wouldn't take kindly to a pathologist sitting on the fence for a month, not when they've got a corpse lying in some ditch.'

They rose and walked through into the lounge for coffee. As they filled their cups from an urn on a side table, Donnington turned his lined, but still handsomely august, face to Hardy.

'How are things going, John? You know what I mean.' As they lowered themselves into a pair of easy chairs around a glass-topped coffee table, John thought carefully of an answer.

'I've only been back a matter of a week or so, James. To be honest, things are not too good. This place – the whole area, I mean – is too full of memories. Jo was part of the scenery, I see her patients in the street every time I go out. The house is empty without her, it echoes as if there's an unlaid ghost there … I don't mean to be over-dramatic, but one can't help listening and suddenly hoping it was all just a nightmare.'

The silver head nodded slowly. 'I know what you mean, John. But it's early days yet. Time heals most things, you know.'

Hardy was silent. The other man was saying all the right things, but there was that something lacking in the bond between them that made them just words. But the second these thoughts crossed his mind, Hardy rebuked himself. It was grossly unfair, he told himself. Donnington was only trying to be helpful, to be kind.

He sighed, watching the bubbles whirl in his coffee as he stirred it.

'I don't know if I'm going to be able to stick it here, James. I already feel that I want to wipe the slate clean, start from scratch somewhere completely different.'

Donnington frowned. 'We'll miss you, John. I'd miss you personally and I'm damned sure the University would miss you, both as a teacher and as a faculty member who would be hard to replace. Don't do anything hasty, give yourself some time.'

Hardy nodded slowly. 'There'll be nothing hasty about it, I assure you. It's not all that easy to pull up your roots, when they're planted as deeply as mine.'

Donnington steered the rather sad conversation into lighter channels and soon it was time for Hardy to get back to chase the histology laboratory for the microscope slides of Joyce Daniel's heart muscle. It was twenty-past two before they were finally produced and, with a forlorn hope, he switched on the light of his microscope and settled down to scan them under the powerful lenses.

The inquest was held in the local Magistrates' Court adjacent to the police station at Norton Heath.

As in any criminal death, no full inquest would be held unless, in the fullness of time, the police failed to charge a suspect with the death. Sometimes they might get a likely candidate, but the Director of Public Prosecutions, in his wisdom, might decide not to bring the case to trial, usually because it looked like a certain loser.

At the moment, it was far too early to classify the Joyce Daniels case either way, but the routine was the same. The coroner held a short 'opening', merely to establish the identity of the deceased and to issue documents for disposal of the body.

Hardy arrived, with his usual punctuality, within a few minutes of four fifteen. The weather had suddenly improved and it was one of those clear, fine autumn days. He stood for a moment in the sun outside the police station and consciously pushed aside all thoughts of death and the complicated rigmarole that civilisation wraps around its investigation. He stood with his briefcase in his hand, idly looking at the passing life of a Midlands town. Anyone watching him might have thought that he was a typewriter repair man or a civil servant from the Department of the Environment. The sun on his face took his mind back to his recent holiday – he wondered where all his fellow passengers on that cruise were at that moment. As his thoughts drifted and the tension relaxed in his muscles, he looked about him at the people on the street.

A fairly respectable vagrant shuffled by, talking earnestly to himself, his worldly possessions carefully wrapped in a brown paper parcel. The old man passed two teenagers standing on the edge of the kerb and Hardy smiled as he recognised the .early stages of courtship that were almost as stereotyped as the love dance of certain birds. The boy was astride his bicycle, leaning across the handlebars until his nose almost touched that of the sixteen-year-old girl, who stood looking over the boy's shoulder with a self-conscious archness, both of them excited at something they didn't quite understand.

Hardy sighed as he turned to go into the building. What would he give to be a teenager again ... or would he? For him, it had been a non-stop marathon of school and university. It seemed marvellous in retrospect, but he had a suspicion that he only remembered the high spots, not all the .times when he had been lonely, unhappy, embarrassed and frustrated. No, unless he could go back with the knowledge and insight of adult life, he would rather settle for today ... or rather, last year.

With a start, he found that he was already standing at the door of the court. He shook himself mentally – *I really must stop this habit of sinking myself in the past*, he thought. *Is this really how old age comes on*? He pushed the door open and walked inside to the inquest. Though Norton Heath was not his immediate hunting ground, he did autopsies quite frequently for Jeremy Kieller, the local coroner, and appeared at his inquests every few months.

The coroner's officer, a rather elderly plain-clothes constable, hurried up to him and ushered him into a seat near the front of the courtroom, with all the ceremony and solicitude of a churchwarden settling down a bishop.

'I'll tell Mr Kieller you're here, Doctor,' he hissed in a stage whisper and hurried his portly body off into the magistrate's room behind the rather garish Royal Coat of Arms that hung over the raised dais.

Hardy, sat quietly in his pew, his hands folded neatly over the thin folder that contained his autopsy report on Joyce Daniels. The last time he had attended an inquest had been as an ordinary witness, he remembered bitterly. The inquest was on his wife, another 'opening' on a criminal death of a woman. There had been no trial of the man who had shot her; his mental state had deteriorated so badly that he was found 'unfit to plead' and was committed to a mental hospital. Which did nothing at all to bring back Jo.

Hardy found his hands clenching painfully on the desk in front of him and he forced himself to relax. To divert himself, he looked around the large room, normally used each day for a multitude of minor offences. Speeding, parking, drinking, domestic quarrels –'all human life was there', as one Sunday paper put it.

The room was far too large for a mere coroner's inquest. At the moment, reporters outnumbered everyone else. Half a dozen of them sat in the pew reserved for the Press. There were three men and a girl from newspapers and another two fellows freelancing for television and the agencies.

On the other end of the row behind him, he saw a hard-faced woman of about fifty with a seedy-looking man sporting large sideburns. He guessed they would be the people who passed as Joyce's next of kin. As he watched, Detective Inspector Williams from Norton Heath came in, looked round and nodded to someone outside the door. Then Lewis Carrol stumped into the court and walked down to sit behind Hardy. Williams slid in alongside Alice, who leaned forward to whisper in Hardy's ear.

'Got anything new for us, Doc?'

Hardy shook his head and craned his neck around.

'Sorry. I've just come from looking at the microscope material. Not a thing, I'm afraid.'

He was glad he couldn't see Alice's expression, but at that moment, the door behind the bench opened. The paternal and self-important PC Herbert came out, reminding Hardy of a cuckoo in a clock, as he threw out his chest and recited the old summons to an inquest.

'Rise for Her Majesty's Coroner!'

As those in court stood up – now joined by a few Nosy Parkers who had slipped in to sit at the back – Jeremy Kieller hurried through the door with a pack of papers under his arm and sat quickly in the large chair normally occupied by the chairman of the magistrates.

The coroner's officer bawled over his head at the sparsely populated court.

'All those who have anything to do touching the death

of Joyce Mary Daniels, draw near and give your attendance.'

Everyone shuffled down into their seats. Jeremy Kieller nodded pleasantly at Hardy and began arranging his papers in front of him. He was a small man with a prematurely lined face, but there was a humour in his mouth that he sometimes had trouble in controlling, especially at the normally sombre proceedings of an inquest. He nodded at his acolyte and PC Herbert grabbed a battered New Testament from the bench and waved it at the sour-faced woman behind Hardy.

'Mrs Lander. Will you come into the box please?' His voice rang through the echoing room as if he was calling a witness across the width of the Old Bailey.

The down-at-heel man next to her gave her a helpful shove and she walked rather reluctantly to the raised oak witness box that stood at one side of the bench. Hardy always thought that it strongly resembled a half-finished garden shed.

The grey-moustached coroner's officer thrust the book at her and held out an oblong of cardboard.

'Take-the-book-in-your-right-hand-and-read-what's-on-the-card.'

He said this as if it were all one word.

Doris Lander mumbled through the oath and then stood fiddling with her handbag, staring uncertainly about the court, her cold eyes flickering from her husband across to the reporters and then back to the coroner.

Mr Kieller turned his corrugated face towards her.

'You are Mrs Doris Lander of eighteen, Waterloo Place, Stoke-on-Trent?'

The woman nodded and said 'Yes' in such a low voice that no one further than PC Herbert could hear her.

'You must speak up, if you would, Mrs Lander. The rest of the people in the court want to hear you.'

The coroner's voice was pleasant, but firm.

'You are the aunt of the deceased girl?'

'Yes, sir. She was my brother's child.'

Her voice was marginally stronger, but the reporters had to strain their ears to catch it.

'I'm sorry to have had to ask you here on such a sad occasion, Mrs Lander, but you realise these things have to be done.'

He paused and peered at her, but there was no response.

'You identified the body at the hospital as that of your niece, Joyce Mary Daniels?'

'Yes, sir. It was Joyce all right.'

Her voice was still a loud whisper, but she seemed to show no obvious signs of grief. Hardy, who had sat through a thousand such painful scenes, knew that the outward signs meant nothing. The most dramatic outbursts could be quite superficial, while the apparently deadpan reactions might conceal a bottomless pit of misery. He had all too recent experiences of his own to confirm this.

Kieller was talking gently to the woman, though how much she took in was a doubtful matter.

'This is not a full inquiry, you understand, Mrs Lander. That will have to come later, either here or in some other court. All we are concerned with today is to know definitely that the unfortunate dead girl was Joyce Daniels and, if we can, to know how she died. Is there anything you can tell us now that might shed any light on that?'

The aunt looked blankly at him.

'Did she have any illnesses that you know of?' prompted the coroner.

Doris Lander shook her head. 'No. She was always fit as a fiddle.'

'Never been in hospital? No diseases run in the family? No sort of heart disease, for instance?'

As he already knew what Hardy was going to say, Mr Kieller was trying to squeeze any useful information from the woman, but there appeared none to squeeze.

'When did you last see her, Mrs Lander?' he asked, after she had shaken her head to the last questions.

'About a year ago, sir. We didn't keep in touch much, not since she came down here.'

There was a note of disapproval in the reply.

The coroner decided that he might be treading on sensitive ground, so he gently dismissed the aunt. She trudged back to her place alongside her husband who, Hardy now noticed, had a disconcerting facial tic that distorted his left eye every few moments.

He was suddenly diverted from this almost hypnotising twitch by PC Herbert's stentorian call.

'Dr John Hardy, please.'

He gathered up his file and climbed the three steps into the witness box.

The coroner's officer placed the New Testament before him with a benign smile, but made no effort to tell him what to do, a subtle acknowledgement of his status.

'I swear by Almighty God that I shall speak the truth, the whole truth and nothing but the truth.'

He always said this slowly and deliberately, trying to sound as if he meant it – which he did, though he was becoming less sure about the reference to the Almighty.

'You are Dr John Hardy, consultant forensic pathologist?'

'I am.'

'And I understand that you performed a post-mortem examination on the body of Joyce Daniels on ... let me see ... October the fourteenth this year?'

'I did.'

'Can you tell me who identified the body to you, Dr Hardy?'

Hardy slid a few sheets of paper out of the file. 'It was not identified to me at the time of the post-mortem, but on the sixteenth, I was present at the mortuary of Norton Heath Hospital when a Miss Sylvia Marsh came back in the presence of police officers – who included Detective Superintendent Partridge – and identified the body as that of Joyce Daniels.'

The coroner wrote on his papers, then came to the awkward part which was a source of embarrassment to them both.

'Now then, Dr Hardy,' he began slowly, unable to resist a quick look under his eyebrows at the poised pencils of the reporters. 'We come to the matter of the cause of death. What can you tell us of that?'

Hardy took a deep breath, not because he was in the slightest way nervous or apprehensive, but this was a matter which had caused him hours of thought and a lot of work.

'I am unable to give a cause of death, sir. There was insufficient discovered at the post-mortem examination to reveal what actually killed the unfortunate girl.'

The coroner, who knew perfectly well what Hardy was going to say next, heard a series of rapid scratching noises from the direction of the Press box, as half a dozen pens and pencils tore across their pads.

'Can you elaborate on that, Doctor? In a mere opening of an inquest like this, we do not require any detail, but in this rather unusual case, perhaps we could have just a little more information.'

Hardy rested both his hands firmly on the edge of the witness box.

'There are a number of possibilities, but none are capable of real proof. The girl might have died from a sudden heart failure – the so-called cardiac arrest, which may have been due to severe shock. This is sometimes seen in criminal abortions, falling into cold water, or even a sudden fright, such as an explosion.'

The coroner had got more than he had expected. 'But none of those conditions could have been present here?' He sounded rather testy.

'Indeed no ... but I was merely using those as examples. There were other possibilities, such as a rather rare heart disease called myocarditis, but I have excluded that on microscopic examination.'

'Are there any other possibilities?'

'A blow to the neck is an outside chance, the so-called "commando punch" or any sort of sudden pressure on the blood vessels there. But one almost always gets bruising or other damage, which was not present here. Some type of suffocation would also be a possibility, though there are no signs of asphyxia.'

Kieller brushed his white hair back with a hand.

'You seem to have demolished each theory as soon as you propose it, Dr Hardy. Any other possibilities?'

'The body has been extensively examined in all possible ways. Laboratory tests for drugs have been carried out, without success, except for a small quantity of alcohol. I must add, sir, that a negative post-mortem examination is by no means unknown. I would estimate that perhaps one to five per cent really provide no satisfactory cause of death, though in older people, there is usually some degree of degeneration, such as coronary artery disease, which can be blamed.'

Kieller twirled a pen around his fingers and stared into the middle distance.

'Yet there are ... well, let us say sinister features about this case which might well indicate foul play. Yet you cannot find a cause of death?'

Hardy inclined his head. 'Exactly so, sir.'

He refused to enlarge upon the matter or to offer any apologies. This told the coroner that in view of the possibility of the case going to a criminal court, it was time to call a halt to further speculation.

'Thank you, Dr Hardy.'

Hardy stepped down and resumed his seat, to the sibilant whispering from the Press box, where the less proficient shorthand writers were cribbing from their colleagues to fill the gaps in their record.

'Detective Chief Superintendent Carrol.'

The coroner's officer seemed to relish the fact that the lowest rank of police officer was for once able to give an order to the highest ranker.

Alice lurched out of his seat and went into the witness box. He still wore his long tweed overcoat. Hardy wondered if he went to bed in it.

After he was sworn in, the coroner had very little discussion with him.

'Chief Superintendent, I understand that though no one has yet been charged with a criminal offence in this case, you are treating it as a possible homicide?'

'We are, sir. There are features that indicate that some crime was committed, even if we are at the moment unable to confirm that a criminal act actually caused the death.'

His bald head rotated until he looked directly down at Hardy, then it swung back again to the coroner.

'In that event, we cannot of course know if the body needs to be retained for examination by the defence, as there naturally is no defence?'

'No, sir.'

'What are the wishes of the police in this direction?'

Carrol turned his palms up in gesture of doubt. 'It's hard to know what to do, sir. Dr Hardy seems to think that no useful purpose can be served by any further examination. And as there seems little likelihood at the moment of any charge being brought, I cannot see how the police could object to burial.'

He stood down and passed Hardy, giving him a look which seemed to say, 'What the hell do we do now?'

Jeremy Kieller brought the proceedings to a rapid close. 'In view of the circumstances, I will issue a burial order to the next of kin. Naturally, there can be no question of cremation until it is definitely established that no criminal proceedings will arise from the death. To allow the police to pursue their enquiries, I will adjourn this inquest for six weeks – though naturally, if such proceedings materialise, that date will have to be further postponed.'

He stood up, scooping his papers together and the ever alert PC Herbert yelled at the assembly to stand, as the coroner vanished into the back room.

Hardy stood up and turned around to talk to the detectives in the row behind. Just at that moment, the swing-doors at the back of the court opened and Sam Partridge appeared, beckoning urgently to Lewis Carrol.

The two senior detectives spoke for a moment, their heads almost touching, then Partridge dived out again.

Alice came striding ponderously down the aisle to where Hardy and the divisional DI were standing.

'Hope you've brought your black bag, Doc. We've got another.'

He swung around and made for the door, beckoning over his shoulder as he went.

Chapter Four

Hardy followed Alice's Austin Maxi and a white police car carrying Sam Partridge. This time, the cavalcade went west out of Norton Heath, towards Redditch and the M5 motorway beyond.

It was open country scattered with commuter villages, market gardens and the odd small factory, signs of the slow but remorseless approach of Birmingham away to the north.

Some seven miles from Norton Heath, the leading police Rover turned off the main road and slowly bumped down a rough track between some scraggy elder trees. The hedges were composed half of unkempt bushes and half of rusted corrugated-iron sheets.

Hardy expected a long, rough ride but, within two hundred yards, the lane turned sharply and they found themselves in an overgrown yard where three more police vehicles stood waiting.

On the further side of the yard was a farmhouse, now semi-derelict with rafters showing through the slates and all the windows smashed.

He pulled up behind the Maxi and got out. A keen wind cut through his suit – he had expected to have spent the time in a heated courtroom, not begin scratching around the countryside in the approaching dusk.

Lewis Carrol came up to him and Sam Partridge joined them. Williams went across to the front of the house to talk to a uniformed chief inspector standing with some other officers.

'Found only an hour ago, Doc,' said Partridge. 'Looks

uncommonly like the same pattern as Joyce Daniels, by all accounts.'

Another car ground along the dirt track and stopped near them. It was Archie Salmon and his liaison officer.

'Here's Einstein,' muttered Alice, banging his cold hands together. 'Be dark in an hour, so they dug him out of the "Forensic" pretty smartly.'

The scientist came across, his usual cheery grin firmly in place. Hardy had always had an urge to pull at that impossible frizz of hair to see if it was a wig or not.

'Business is good these days, lads,' commented Archie. 'What have you got for us today, Alice?'

'Tell 'em, Sam,' grunted Carrol, turning to look at the half-ruined farm.

The detective superintendent pointed at the downstairs windows.

'About three o'clock, two youths with air rifles came past here with a dog. They were going after rats or rabbits or some damn thing. They intended going on past the farmhouse, down the lane to some fields beyond. But the dog suddenly goes spare and dashes into the house, barking like hell.'

He indicated a gaping doorway between the two downstairs bay windows. The battered door lay drunkenly off one hinge, falling backwards into the gloom of the passage.

'They thought the pooch might have raised some rats, so, for the fun of it, they went in after him – and came out a damned sight faster than they'd entered. The dog was barking and scratching at something lying under a corrugated sheet in the left-hand room off the hall. They pulled the sheet aside and saw the body of a girl. Dropped everything and ran back to a phone box up the road, dialled 999. That's about it.'

Hardy looked across at the house and then at the dark clouds overhead that were threatening both rain and an early dusk.

'Anything been done so far?'

Some brilliant blue flashes from the house answered part of his question.

'Photographers have just about finished. We got the local police surgeon just to certify death, but he said he wasn't getting mixed up in it any deeper if you were on your way, Doc.'

Alice looked at his henchman. 'Everything set up, Sam? We can use the room at Norton Heath for this as well, if Dr Hardy here can oblige us, this time.'

The sarcasm was heavy, but Hardy smiled politely at him and felt the better for not taking offence.

They all set off for the grim front entrance of the old house. A uniformed PC was standing there, again with a clipboard and register of entrants.

'Don't let anyone in without asking me first,' Alice said sternly to the sentinel. 'Not even the bleeding Chief Constable. We get too many people rubbernecking on these scenes, putting their big feet where they shouldn't.'

With a ferocious scowl on his face, he moved inside, stepping delicately with his big body, watching the ground in front of him.

Hardy followed him and saw that the little passage was cluttered with rubble and broken slates. Above him, he could see through the shattered floor to the roof, itself peppered with holes.

'In here, Doc. Not room to swing a cat, so I'll stay at the door.'

Hardy looked carefully through the gaping doorway into the ruin of a room. The ceiling had gone completely and there was a heap of rotten joists, masonry, slates and plaster in the middle of the floor. Not only the wreckage of the house, but a lot of gratuitous garbage thrown in by rubbish dumpers, both through the door and via the frameless window.

As he looked, two Special Incident Squad men appeared outside the window and set up the large gas lamp, probably the same one that he had seen in the wood the other night. The white flare filled the room and the approaching dusk was banished instantly.

'What a bloody mess!' muttered Archie from behind his shoulder. The laboratory man, dressed in a hairy sports coat and corduroy trousers, gazed around the derelict room, his eyes taking in the rotten mattress near the door, a heap of empty wine bottles, a scatter of sodden paper and a general leavening of what appeared to be the contents of half a dozen dustbins.

'She's over there, lads,' said Lewis Carrol from the door. He pointed to the far corner, diagonally opposite to where they had entered the room.

Hardy hesitated. There was such a lot of material between him and the corner that he was bound to kick and squash some of it as he moved. His instincts told him that anything there might be vital to the investigation, but short of flying, he had no choice.

Alice seemed to read his mind. 'I know, Doc, but we've got to lump it, I'm afraid. A few people have trodden across already, so try to keep to the same line.'

With Archie behind him, he tiptoed across the room, 'like a pair of bloody Indians on the trail', as Carrol later described it over a pint in the Police Club.

A rusty sheet of corrugated iron leaned drunkenly against the far wall, where it had been placed by the first lad to find the body. He had moved it along a couple of feet, as Carrol said that the boys told the police it had originally been completely hiding the body.

As it was now, a pair of still, white legs protruded from behind the sheet, close against the crumbling plaster of the old wall. Rubbish lay all around and the legs actually rested on a rotting sack that spilled empty jam jars onto the wet ground.

'We can't see much with this flaming tin here,' complained Archie.

'Can we move it now?' asked Hardy, over his shoulder.

Carrol came across to Sam and Evan Williams, who stood outside the gaping window, alongside the light.

'Have we got all the pictures, Sam?'

'Yes, from here, sir. Mostyn is trying to climb up onto the rafters to get a shot downwards of the whole room.'

'Watch he doesn't break his bloody neck, then,' growled Alice.

He took a step into the room to get a better view. 'OK, Archie, pull the sheet away, but we haven't had the fingerprint boys here yet so play it clever, will you.'

The wild-looking biologist bent down and placed the fingers of one hand flat under the bottom edge of the corrugated iron. The other hand he rested in the same fashion on the top edge, so as not to put the pads of his fingers on the face of the metal. Carefully, he lifted it clear of the floor and turned it vertically instead of lying lengthwise. He carefully rotated his body and rested the rusty sheet against an adjacent wall, well away from the corpse.

'That's better, let the dog see the rabbit.'

He stood alongside Hardy and they both looked down at the floor at their feet.

'Poor girl,' said Hardy sympathetically. The words were simple, but his feelings were deep. Unlike the quarry victim, one glance was enough to show the probable cause of death.

The body was that of a girl lying face down on the floor, but with sufficient of her neck and chin showing to reveal the tell-tale signs of asphyxia. Hardy knelt down and looked almost from floor level at her face. He saw blood oozing from her nostrils and the pink-purple colour of the skin, dotted with small blotches and pinprick haemorrhages.

This time the arms were held crookedly in front of the head, as if in some clumsy dive. The legs were straight out behind, covered to the knees by a bright red skirt, now smeared with the dirt from the derelict house.

Hardy climbed to his feet and absently dusted off the front of his trouser legs. Then he stood alongside Archie and stared silently at the body.

'Well, what's the score?' Lewis Carrol called, rather impatiently, from near the door. He could not see much from there, because of the two figures blocking his view, as well as the mound of rubbish in the middle of the room.

'You'd better come across, Mr Carrol,' suggested Hardy. 'We'll need some photographs before I do much more.'

Alice picked his way delicately across to them and looked at the girl.

'Poor lass. Looks the same sort of job as the other one.'

John Hardy scanned the body from end to end.

'Asphyxia, I'm sure. Though from what, I don't yet know.'

'Do you see what I see, John,' asked Archie, pointing down.

'Yes, the wrists again. Must be the same johnny as last time.'

Hardy crouched near the head of the girl and looked at her arms. He vividly remembered doing the same thing with Joyce Daniels. Around both wrists there was a clear-cut reddish band on the skin, about an inch wide.

'Not cord or wire, Archie. Looks more like a strap.'

The biologist held his torch very near the arms. 'Yes, look there. A line across, just as if the bar of a buckle had cut into the surface.'

Alice looked around at the debris scattered all about them. 'We'd better search all this lot pretty thoroughly. Could be half a dozen straps hidden in this lot.'

There was a scuffling above them and a shower of grit

and plaster rattled into the corner of the room. It was the police photographer who had scrambled up from outside and was now perched precariously on the remains of the joists that had once been the bedroom floor.

'Watch it, my lad. Don't kick any more of that muck down here. And don't fall down yourself.'

There began a series of brilliant flashes as the man took a dozen photographs of the scene below. The trio near the body moved away to give him a clear field. When he had finished, Hardy suggested that he took some close-ups of the body from ground level, before they disturbed it.

'May as well pull out and leave him to it for ten minutes, said Carrol.

As they turned to move out, Hardy's restless eyes scanned the heap of rubbish that lay next to the girl. Something attracted his attention and, later, he thought that it was probably because the object was much cleaner than the surrounding junk.

He saw a plastic bag, about eighteen inches square, lying crumpled on the mound of rotten timber, old tins and broken glass. It was an ordinary clear polythene bag, the sort that might be used to wrap sandwiches, though rather bigger. He bent to look at it as he moved to the door. Something else caught his attention.

'Archie, have you got a torch with you?'

The forensic scientist pulled a torch from the pocket of his jacket and shone the beam downwards.

'What are you looking at, John?'

'That bag. Looks quite fresh. What's that inside it, stuck to the inner surface?'

Archie went right down with his torch, to augment the bright, but more diffuse light from the gas lamp.

'Blood ... blood and mucus, by the look of it. Well, well!'

'We must have that. But get a photograph first. Mr Carrol, this may be important.'

He called Alice back from the front door and pointed out the bag.

'For heaven's sake keep that, after we've got a picture of it.'

The chief superintendent's face wrinkled like an old prune.

'You've got a "cause" for us this time, Doc?'

Hardy nodded. 'We may have a cause for the last one, too, if it's the same chap with the same habits.'

Alice's face cracked into a devilish grin.

'Monty Lever! ' he growled. 'If we nail him, Doc, I'll buy you a pint.'

This time, the body arrived at the mortuary at the civilised hour of six in the evening. It also arrived in style, having been picked up by an undertaker in a plain blue Morris van.

Hardy had left the scene about half an hour after the bag had been found and went ahead to the hospital five miles away, where the coroner's officer had arranged for the post-mortem to be carried out. They were still in the area of the coroner who had held the inquest that afternoon, so the urbane PC Herbert was the man who smoothed the path of the investigation. He had the manner of a master of ceremonies or a grand vizier. When Hardy arrived at the mortuary he was waiting outside to direct his car to a convenient parking place and insisted on holding the door of the car open like a footman at Claridges.

'You've used this mortuary before, Doctor?' he enquired.

Hardy nodded as he looked around in the dusk. The hospital was a Victorian monstrosity of dull red brick and as usual, the mortuary was the smallest building hidden in

the furthest corner of the grounds. It huddled between the boiler house and the compound where the refuse bins were kept, a little building crouching apologetically against a high wall.

Herbert shepherded Hardy inside, where things were just as he remembered them from the last time he used the place. The outer room was half-filled with a refrigerator holding four bodies. The rest of the space was cluttered by galvanised trolleys for wheeling the dead, various buckets, squeegees and mops and the mortuary keeper's bicycle.

The inner sanctum, more brilliantly lit by one fluorescent light, was the post-mortem room proper. It was lined by antique, chipped white tiles, which rose to an old-fashioned glass cupola. In the centre was a massive porcelain autopsy table. Some cupboards, a sink, a small desk in the corner and more assorted oddments completed the equipment.

'The mortuary chap has gone off to Manchester to his daughter's wedding,' said PC Herbert. 'So I'll officiate for you, sir.'

And this he did, with great style, wearing his lovat trilby hat throughout his ministrations as Hardy's assistant.

The sound of the van outside sent them to put on white operating gowns, rubber boots, gloves and heavy green rubber aprons, secured round the neck and waist by brass chains. Hardy thought that the equipment, like the building, was probably old at the time of the relief of Mafeking.

As Hardy stood waiting for the police and the body to come inside, he thought wistfully of the meal he had promised himself that evening. Since his return, he had resolved to fend for himself as far as meals were concerned. He intended to return to his bachelor prowess with saucepan and grill, but so far he had managed it only on a handful of occasions, making do with a large lunch at the University and just a snack at night. Often he took the coward's way out by going out to dine in the evening.

His job never interfered with his appetite and, as he waited for the corpse to be slid onto the big table, his stomach told him by various rumbles that it had been neglected for too many hours.

Again wrapped in polythene, the girl now lay under the harsh fluorescent tube. Carrol, Partridge, Salmon and a few other police officers, including the photographers and liaison officer, soon filled the tiny room until it seemed bursting with large men.

Archie Salmon put on a pair of gloves and an apron and assembled his battery of bottles, packets and tubes on a small table.

Hardy used his own instruments for the post-mortem, taken from his bag which he laid on the top of an antiquated glass cupboard filled with a scatter of surgical gadgets that looked as if they had been excavated from some archaeological dig.

Evan Williams, the silent detective inspector, volunteered to take notes for Hardy, who had not brought his pocket dictating machine, having been called straight from the inquest.

Archie and Hardy carefully unfolded the polythene to reveal the body, still dressed in the red skirt and a lurex-threaded black evening jumper.

'Been on the town, by the looks of it,' commented Carrol. 'You don't go to work in Woolworths or the gas office in that rig-out.'

Hardy stood back again while the man-made lightning of the camera's electronic flash recorded the clothed body on film. Then the man from the Home Office laboratory went all over the exposed skin with strips of Sellotape, to pick up any tiny particles that might be matched later with something from the assailant. He next combed the hair out into a basin and preserved some small fragments in an envelope.

The hair was rather inexpertly dyed an auburn shade, though the brown roots gave away the true colour.

'About twenty-five, you reckon?' asked Partridge. 'Bit older than Joyce Daniels.'

Hardy nodded. The woman was still young, but even in death, she looked rather harder and more experienced. There was dirt and bits of rubbish adhering to the face and the discoloration of asphyxia was heightened by the gravitational settling of blood into the skin of the face.

They carefully undressed her, putting each garment into separately-labelled plastic bags. These were carefully recorded by the Exhibits Officer, one of the 'Scenes of Crime' detectives whose job it was to see that all evidence was strictly accounted for, right up to the time of the trial, if there was to be one.

'No pants again, just like the last one,' said Archie thoughtfully, as he dropped a pair of torn tights into a bag.

'The tights were not pulled up properly, notice that?' said Hardy.

Apart from a brassiere, there were no underclothes and now the girl lay white and naked under the cold light. A dozen pairs of eyes stared at her, but there was not one mind that thought of her as a sexual object, only in the sense that this was probably the victim of a sexual crime.

Hardy then went meticulously over every inch of skin looking for and recording any abnormality, scratch, bruise or cut. The eyes, mouth, ears, nostrils, breasts, genitals, hands and feet were examined minutely. He dictated monotonously to the DDI who was writing it all down for him.

When he had finished, he took a long thermometer from a cardboard tube in his case and slipped it deeply into the back passage, which he had already examined.

While he was waiting the required minute for the mercury to reach its final level, he stood back and clasped his rubber-sheathed fingers across the waist of his apron.

'So far, Mr Carrol, we've got a girl undoubtedly dead from asphyxia. Congestion of the face, haemorrhages into the eyelids, skin around the mouth, eyes and cheeks … no doubt at all. No marks on the neck, so she wasn't strangled. But if my reading of that plastic bag is correct, it was over her head at some stage. And of course, the tying of the arms puts it right in the same court as the last one.'

Alice's eyes gleamed. 'And what about Joyce Daniels?'

'Could have been exactly the same thing. Smothering – or at least, sudden obstruction of the mouth and nose – needn't cause any asphyxial signs. But proving it is next to impossible, except by inference from another case such as this one.'

Hardy turned away to look at the level on his thermometer. He stood for a moment, doing some mental arithmetic.

'Within the last day, probably inside the sixteen to twenty-two hour bracket, considering the temperature in that old house. Again, you can put a few hours on either end of that range and still be within possible limits.'

Another few minutes were taken up with the final external examination. Hair and eyebrow samples were obtained and pubic hair was also put into Archie's little plastic jars. The nails were clipped short, each finger into ten separate containers. Scrapings were taken of lipstick and the remains of make-up on the cheeks, all in case they needed to be compared with traces on the clothing or belongings of a suspect.

Again recent sexual intercourse was obvious, though there seemed to be no definite signs of violence associated with it.

Satisfied at last, John Hardy turned to his willing acolyte, Constable Herbert, who stood in his green apron and trilby, a selection of knives in his hand.'

The next hour separated the men from the boys and several of the younger detectives and uniformed policemen found it nicer in the cold fresh air outside. Methodically, Hardy worked through every organ, looking for signs of injury or natural disease.

At about seven thirty he threw down his knife and

peeled off his gloves.

'That's it, Mr Carrol. A bit more definite than last time!'

As he washed his hands, the coroner's officer began repairing the wreckage that had once been an attractive woman. At the sink, Hardy gave a summary of his findings to the investigating officers.

'Asphyxiated, almost certainly by that plastic bag. There are traces of blood and mucus from the nose inside it. Archie here will do the necessary tests to check the blood groups and verify that the mucus came from the mouth or nasal passages. No other signs of injury. She's had sex recently, there's obviously semen present. Again it will be very interesting to see what group it is.'

Sam Partridge clapped his hands loudly. 'If it's not Group B, I'll give up and go and breed chickens.'

Lewis Carrol nodded vigorously. 'I'll be off home to pray tonight, too. Pray that we can catch this bastard Lever this time. His luck can't hold this far. Cheeky devil, trying it on twice in a week.'

'If it's him, he must be going round the twist. Psychopathic sex killer,' said Archie Salmon. 'Why has he suddenly gone sadistic like this?'

Hardy was more cautious. 'Don't jump your fences too quickly. There are differences between the two deaths. No rape, it looks like voluntary intercourse. The first one got a lot of publicity, maybe some mentally deranged chap decided to add to the local murder rate.'

Carrol looked dubious. 'Don't cut the ground from under your own feet, Doc. What about the plastic bag side of it?'

Hardy nodded as he began taking off his gown. 'I'll admit, the plastic bag theory would take a weight off my mind as far as Joyce Daniels is concerned. Asphyxia was one of the things I mentioned at the inquest, you remember.'

Alice grabbed Sam Partridge by the arm. 'I think we'll be having a little talk with Monty Lever now, Sam,' he said.

By nine o'clock, they knew who the girl was. Detective Inspector Williams, the one who had written the notes for Hardy, went to the Saracen Club and spoke to the barman.

'Did you have a girl in here last night, dyed red hair, about twenty-five? Wearing a black lurex jumper and a red skirt.'

'Sounds like Penny … Penny Vincent.' The barman put down a bottle he was holding and craned his neck to look around the dimly lit club. It was early and only a dozen or so people were in there.

'She don't seem to be here yet,' he said.

'Maybe she never will be again,' answered the DDI. He told the barman to get his coat and a few minutes later they were driving towards the mortuary.

Forty minutes later, the detective team met in the murder room at the police station.

Sam Partridge did most of the talking at first. 'We've definitely identified the victim as Penny Vincent. She's supposed to be a part-time barmaid, but she spends every evening in the clubs. What you might charitably call a "freelance hostess". Inspector Williams here knows her, I think.'

The self-effacing DI added to what was known of the girl.

'Not exactly on the game, but I'd say she was an enthusiastic amateur, not above taking a few quid unless she really fancied the chap. She works out of both Lever's clubs and some others nearer Brum. No form, as far as I know, but she's certainly on the road to being a tart.'

'How old was she?' asked Carrol.

'I'm not sure. The barman in the Saracen says she's supposed to be twenty-four, but I think you can add a couple of years on to that. She's certainly been around. A hard-bitten little bird, she was.'

'Never speak ill of the dead!' said Partridge.

'I want a team in the club getting a statement from everyone there. Bar staff, girls, customers ... everyone,' snapped Carrol. 'Then I want a house-to-house all around that old farm, seeing if anyone heard a vehicle, anything unusual ... what the hell, you know the drill!'

'And Monty Lever ... where does he come into this?' asked Partridge.

'Bloody quick ... as soon as we find where he is, we want him down here "helping us with our enquiries" ... and tell him to bring his bed with him, he'll need it, the time he's going to be here.'

But Lever was not so easy to get.

They found him quickly enough, for he was in the Saracen all the time. One of the upstairs rooms was an office, used mainly by Dickie Durrant, the Manager. But several times a week, Monty Lever came there to collect the takings and to look at Durrant's accounts – both the private ones and those they kept for the Inland Revenue. Not infrequently, Lever would use the room to entertain a girl. Then Durrant would be exiled to sit downstairs at the bar, plotting ways to get his own club and be free from the tyranny of his master.

This particular night, Williams had just taken the barman back to the Saracen. The employee was distinctly white around the gills after his visit to the hospital mortuary. He poured himself a large whisky and when Williams declined one, said, 'I don't know what the boss is going to say about this.'

'Which boss?' asked the Detective Inspector.

'Both of 'em. Dicky and the Big Chief.'

'Monty Lever? Where is he, then?'

The barman's reply sent the DDI hurrying back to the telephone. 'He's upstairs, right now – the fellow in the bar says Lever was sitting here last night with Penny, as bold as brass!'

Probably the shock of seeing a dead body had loosened up the man's tongue, for only in an unguarded moment would one of Lever's employees have let drop such a juicy bit of news.

But it was too late to pull it back and Evan Williams had phoned it in to the police station before the man had realised what damage he might have done.

Fifteen minutes later, two police cars drew up outside the club and Lewis Carrol, supported by four CID men and two uniformed constables, came into the club.

Dickie Durrant, who had by then been tipped off by the barman, met them at the door, not knowing whether to be belligerent or co-operative.

Alice wasn't bothered how he felt.

'Is Lever upstairs?' he snapped.

When Durrant nodded his head, Carrol detailed a detective sergeant to look after him.

'Take a statement from him. His movements during the last thirty-six hours, anything he knows about the girl … now.'

He turned left inside the foyer and padded up the red-carpeted stairs, Williams in close pursuit. Durrant stood open-mouthed at the bottom, but the sergeant pulled him by the arm to a table.

The upstairs was divided into a number of rooms, some of which were suspected by the police of being used occasionally for a variety of illegal purposes, though so far, Durrant had not been caught red-handed.

At the back of the passage, there was a door with a small notice saying 'Office'.

Carrol knocked with one hand and turned the handle with the other, simultaneously. But it was locked. He hammered loudly with his knuckles.

'Go to hell!' came a voice from inside.

'Police officers,' yelled Carrol, equally loudly. He wondered whether Lever knew what was going on outside.

'Did Durrant get a chance to tip him off?' he asked Williams.

The Welshman shook his head. 'I don't think so. The barman told Dickie, but I sat on them until you came. I don't think they tipped the wink to anyone else'

Alice bashed on the door again with his fist. There was the sound of a chain being released on the inside and then the door swung open.

A man appeared in the doorway. He was big, but podgy, and had a light brown beard and over-long hair to match.

'Oh God, it's you again. I've got nothing more to say.'

Lever started to push the door shut, but Lewis Carrol jammed a huge foot in the gap.

'I want you to come down to the police station, Lever – now!'

Monty Lever's wet lips sneered. 'You must be joking. Take your foot out of my door and go away. I told you all I wished to say, last week.'

Carrol leaned on the door panel and his weight slowly edged it wider against Lever's attempts to shut it.

'Did I say this was anything to do with that?' he asked.

Lever suddenly released the door and Carrol staggered, which did not increase his love for the club owner.

Williams, looking through the now wide-open door, saw a girl sitting on a settee in the room, a glass in her hand.

'You can see that I'm entertaining. Will you please go away or I'll call my solicitor.'

Alice fixed him with a pair of flinty eyes.

'You spent part of last evening in the company of a girl called Penny Vincent.'

It was a statement, not a question.

There was not a flicker on Monty's face.

'Penny? So what? Has she made any complaints?'

A funny answer, thought Williams. He turned sideways and scribbled a record of what was being said.

'What's he writing down?' demanded Lever, his pointed beard wagging in indignation. As usual, he was dressed in a snappy suit, with rounded lapels and a waistcoat to match. His beard ran upwards in a fringe around his chin to join bushy sideburns. His eyes were pale and expressionless, but it was that loose, flabby mouth that made him look so repulsive to Williams.

The girl inside had twigged that something was wrong. She was standing up, staring at them.

'What's the matter, Monty?' she called.

'Sit down and shut up!' he snarled, turning his head momentarily.

'Look, I'm not standing here arguing all night,' snapped Carrol. 'I want you down at the station to answer some questions, Lever. In case you don't know, Penny Vincent is dead. She's been murdered, just like Joyce Daniels was murdered.'

Lever stood stock still in the doorway.

'That's nothing to do with me,' he said shortly.

'I want to ask you some questions. You were with her last night.'

'I've nothing to say. You bloody police are persecuting me. You'll regret it.' He ran a fleshy tongue over his pink lips.

Carrol's jaw quivered and for an awful minute, Williams thought he was going to cry.

'I want you down at the station. Are you coming without trouble?'

Lever suddenly seemed to draw on some internal strength. He straightened his shoulders - which made him as big as Alice – and glared at the police officers.

'I am not coming, no! I have nothing to say. If you want me to come with you, you'll have to arrest me. And

I'll still say nothing, unless my solicitor advises me to do so. Get that?'

He stood defiantly, challenging Carrol to do something about it. Alice knew he had been stalemated – at least for the present. He had no power to make the man go to the station or even to answer the most simple questions. Only if he arrested him and charged him with an offence could he take him away and even then, he would have to be cautioned that he need not say anything unless he wished.

'You're being very unwise, Lever,' said Carrol, slowly.

'*Mister* Lever, to you. And good night!'

He closed the door and the chief superintendent, though seething with anger, had no option but to take his foot out of the door.

'Come on, Williams. We'll get the bastard before the night's through. We just want enough to slap a charge on him. Let's see what the lads downstairs have dug up for us.'

As they trod the thick carpet away from the door, Williams jerked a thumb over his shoulder.

'Best keep an eye on that dame in there, sir. We don't want him attempting the hat-trick later on tonight.'

Chapter Five

Two days later, John Hardy was alone in the laboratory at his home, having forced himself to take an interest in unfinished tasks there. After lunch, he had gone into the silent room, full of good intentions to carry on where he had left off a dozen weeks before.

He wandered around between the benches, running a fastidious finger along the dust on the working surfaces. His daily woman confined her activities to the house and, on Hardy's instructions, had kept clear of the laboratory.

The place was looking distinctly neglected after all this time and Hardy, unable to ignore anything but perfection when it came to working conditions, found some dusters in a drawer and rubbed down one bench to give himself a decent patch on which to work.

The physical activity pleased him, even though the vigorous rubbing made him a little out of breath. He felt that, at last, he was actually doing something, rather than mooning about feeling sorry for himself.

His work at the University was only part-time and most afternoons he devoted to reading, writing scientific papers or working on private cases in his laboratory.

Since Jo's death and his long trip abroad, all this other work had fallen by the wayside. His technical assistant, Sandra, had found herself another job and, until he decided on his future plans, there was little point in looking for a replacement.

But there were things he could get on with in the meantime. A particular interest of his was the study of skeletons, both from the forensic and the archaeological point of view. He was frequently asked to examine bones recovered from a variety of unlikely places, both by the police and by antiquarians and museum authorities. More as a hobby than a professional need, he had developed an interest in the dating of these macabre remains. He tried to estimate when the owner of the bones had died, which could be anything between six months and six thousand years ago.

Boxes and bags of bones were hidden away in the cupboards under his benches, neglected now for a number of months.

A letter which arrived that morning was the real stimulus for him to go to one of these cupboards and pull out a plastic sack containing scores of broken bones, sent in by a museum in the West Country. The letter had been from the University of Oxford; whose archaeologists knew of Hardy's publications on bones and were inviting him to come and discuss the possibility of a research grant, the amount of which made his eyebrows lift.

It was a very tempting offer and he had already written back to arrange a meeting at Oxford to talk the matter through.

His conscience was pricking him now, as lately he had let the whole research project drop due to his personal troubles. Getting the sack of bones out of the cupboard was a propitiation to fate, a token that he would get on with things again.

Hardy put the bag on the recently cleaned bench and gently picked out all the crumbling brown sticks that had once been several human beings.

The first job was to make a count of any identifiable bones to see how many individuals there were. The skeletons, all jumbled together, had been ploughed up in a field in Somerset and the museum wanted to get some idea of their origins. Perhaps it was a Bronze Age barrow that had been reduced to ground level by the plough many years before – maybe it was some medieval battlefield or even one from the Dark Ages. Hardy smiled gently as the thought passed through his mind that the site where they were found was not far from South Cadbury – the Camelot of King Arthur.

He had promised the museum – how long ago he felt too ashamed to think – that he would examine the bones, estimate the number of people represented by them, try to get some idea of the age and sex of the individuals, look for any signs of injury or disease and attempt to put a date to them. The last part was his particular interest and it involved a whole battery of chemical and physical tests. These still gave only the roughest estimate – for example, he could probably tell if they were fifty, five hundred, or a couple of thousand years old, but not much more accurately than that.

With the complacent glow of righteous and honest toil spreading over him, he began to look at each bone and place it on the bench according to the part of the body it came from. He soon had three pelvic bones, four thigh bones, five forearm bones, three lower jaws and many shattered pieces of skull.

As the big, easily identifiable bones began to vanish from the general pile, the going got harder and he had to get down his thick *Gray's Anatomy* from the bookshelf to identify some smaller, broken fragments. Occasionally, he came across a curious bone that by no stretch of imagination could be found anywhere in the book. It was very obviously animal in origin so, for the time being, it went back into the empty bag. With something like this to occupy him, he became oblivious of both time and his own troubles, but he was suddenly brought back to harsh reality by the insistent ringing of the telephone.

This time, he had switched it through to the laboratory extension and as he went towards it he cursed Alexander Graham Bell for inventing the damned thing. How nice it must have been, he thought, for the researchers of the Renaissance, to be free of all interruptions except for the occasional messenger bringing them a civilised parchment couched in classical Latin.

'Hello. John Hardy,' he said, with as good a grace as he could muster.

'John, it's James here, James Donnington.'

Hardy listened to the Dean of Medicine for a long minute.

'Well, of course, I'll give him every assistance, James. The coroner is the man to actually give permission, but that's a matter for the defence solicitor to arrange.'

He listened again, looking wistfully across the laboratory to where his bones were lying waiting on the bench.

'No, I'm afraid I don't know of him. But then, India is a long way off … certainly, I'll look forward to hearing from him. Bye, James, thanks for letting me know.'

Hardy put the phone down and stood pondering for a moment, his fingers restlessly massaging his chin. Who the devil was Professor Sir Glanville West? Should he know?

Walking through to his study, he took down last year's Medical Directory, the second volume 'M-Z', and thumbed through until he came to 'West'.

'West, Philip Glanville, Knight Commander of the British Empire,' he murmured aloud, 'Qualified Cambridge and Middlesex Hospital, 1929.' He looked up and did some mental calculations. 'Twenty-nine? Good God, he must be at least seventy-one now.'

His eyes went back to the red book. 'Colonial Medical Service … Delhi … Rangoon, Darjeeling … Professor of Pathology, Kistna Medical College, Madras, retired 1972.' There were further details and an address at a London club. Professor Sir Glanville West was obviously an ex-bulwark of the British Raj, who was now enjoying – or should have been enjoying – a well-earned retirement back in the land of his birth.

But he was coming tomorrow morning to perform a second post-mortem examination on the body of Penny Vincent, with the object of advising the defence lawyers of Monty Lever, who was languishing in a Birmingham prison.

'Christ, is this chap for real, Doc?' Sam Partridge whispered hoarsely. He was standing with John Hardy outside the mortuary next day, watching Professor Sir Glanville West in earnest conversation with a fat man in a black jacket and grey striped trousers. This was Saul Bannerman, the solicitor representing Monty Lever. The ex-colonial pathologist was just too good to be true, agreed Hardy, though his overdeveloped sense of manners prevented him from saying so to the detective superintendent.

Sir Glanville looked like a stage English colonel, escaped from a West End farce. He was beanpole thin, had a large white moustache and was dressed in a light grey suit, surely bought in Bombay some time prior to 1936. He sported a carnation and wore a wide-brimmed trilby that might have been useful in keeping off the Madras sun, but which looked incongruous in the Midland smog.

He was talking animatedly to Bannerman, his lean, leathery face looking all the more sun-baked for the bushy white eyebrows and white hair that was just visible under the large hat.

'Thank God he hasn't got a monocle and silver-topped walking stick, or I'd run him in for a phoney,' grunted Partridge, who was there to represent the police at the second autopsy.

Hardy had come mainly out of courtesy to the defence pathologist, as he always felt the first post-mortem made such a disruption of the evidence that it was only fair that he should be on hand to explain what the original appearances were like.

Monty Lever had been charged with murder on the day following the episode when he had refused to accompany Lewis Carrol to the police station for questioning. That morning, the forensic laboratory had confirmed that the blood inside the plastic bag was of the same blood group as the dead girl. They also found that the seminal fluid in her body was again the unusual Group B, which had been found in Joyce Daniels and was that of Monty Lever. ·

The man had produced alibis for most of the night in question from his employees and henchmen in the Saracen Club, but the police found several witnesses to confirm that he had spent some time with Penny Vincent in the bar of the club that night.

Though the evidence at that stage was circumstantial and far from watertight, Lewis Carrol decided to charge Lever with murder and he was remanded next day by the magistrates.

His podgy but highly efficient lawyer, Bannerman, had forbidden his client to say anything but a terse denial. The solicitor had then rapidly cast about for a second medical opinion, as it was obvious that no expense was to be spared in challenging anything and everything the prosecution alleged. It was to be a tooth-and-nail struggle all the way – everyone recognised that from the start. Saul Bannerman specialised in 'knocking the police' on all possible occasions. He was the lawyer to a number of Midlands club owners, as well as to a legion of 'fringe operators' who trod the tightrope between legality and crime in all manner of activities, from dubious financial dealings to outright rackets.

Strangely enough, Bannerman was able to pursue this shady line of law practice and still make it quite compatible with an unsullied personal social life. He golfed at the best club, belonged to any number of eminently respectable societies and had a wide range of. upright – and often influential – friends. One of these was James Donnington, Hardy's academic superior. It was Donnington, in fact, who suggested to the solicitor that Sir Glanville might act as the defence pathologist.

'Apparently he knew him years ago in India,' Hardy told Partridge, as they waited for the defence team to finish their discussion.

'I remember now that the Dean spent some time there before the war, teaching in a Medical College. Must have come across West in those days. '

The retired professor now lived in a country house near Evesham and had been driven up in a hired chauffeur-driven car.

'Bloody typical!' marvelled Sam Partridge when he saw it arrive. 'Wonder he didn't come in a howdah on the back of a flaming elephant.'

Eventually, the lawyer brought Sir Glanville across to the mortuary door and introduced him to Hardy and the police officer. Bannerman looked too jovial to be the known police-hater and champion of villains that Hardy knew him to be. He had an almost cherubic face, but the eyes gave away the tempered steel underneath. They were like iced diamonds, cold and forever flashing restlessly about, looking for the best position, any advantage, any edge over the other man.

Introductions were made and some limp handshakes exchanged, then Hardy led the ex-professor inside. The lawyer had done his bit and excused himself, to drive off in his brand new Bentley to the aid of some other crook in trouble.

John Hardy did all he could to be pleasant and obliging to the other doctor, but soon found it to be hard going. His own nature was one of punctilious good manners – Hardy was a gentleman first and everything else came after. Sir Glanville seemed to model himself more upon the feudal system, in which he was the lord and everyone else was a serf. He got off on the wrong foot right away, as they were putting on their gowns.

'James Donnington tells me that you're the full-time medico-legal wallah.'

His voice suits the Indian colonel image too, thought Hardy, though it was quite firm, considering the old boy was well past seventy.

'Yes, I do forensic medicine at the University.'

Sir Glanville nodded condescendingly.

'I suppose there's a place for that, Hardy. I was a *proper* pathologist, of course. Forty-two years of it.'

If the older man had spent his forty-two years devising the most insulting thing to say to Hardy, he could not have succeeded better. Hardy felt the blood throbbing into his face and his stout neck seemed to swell inside the operating gown. He kept his temper with difficulty, screwing down a retort in deference to the other's age and the newness of their acquaintance.

'I was a clinical pathologist myself for six years, Professor,' he managed to say without spitting fire at the same time. 'I think a forensic pathologist *is* a 'proper' pathologist, but one with a particular leaning in one direction.'

The Knight of the British Empire seemed to have lost interest in the subject.

'What an awful place,' he said, looking around the scruffy mortuary.

Hardy secretly agreed with him, but again felt it damned bad taste to immediately complain about a place where he was a mere visitor. They went into the inner room, where the mortuary attendant, now back from his daughter's nuptials, had already got the remains of Penny Vincent laid out on the massive china slab.

She had been refrigerated since the first autopsy and was in good condition. Only the long line of stitching down the body showed that anything had been done previously.

'I'm afraid I can't give you a copy of my report, Sir Glanville, though I'm sure that your instructing solicitor will get a copy through the proper channels. But I can tell you verbally what I found.'

This was the usual routine in these circumstances. The defence doctor was retained by the solicitors of the accused to check on the facts put forward by the prosecution and to make his own interpretation of them.

In most cases, there was no conflict about the facts – if a person was stabbed, then it would be rare for this to be challenged. But matters of opinion might be slanted differently, such as the direction, the force and the depth of the wound. Often, there was complete agreement and the defence pathologist told his lawyers that there was nothing he could offer them to dispute the prosecution evidence. Hardy himself frequently did defence cases and enjoyed the full co-operation of almost all his colleagues up and down the country.

But the imperious Sir Glanville would have none of these gentlemanly tactics. He tartly declined Hardy's offer of assistance.

'It's good of you, Hardy, but I prefer to make my own way. You mustn't tell me a thing! Not proper, you know. Not proper at all.'

Hardy prided himself on his self-composure, but he later vowed that he gaped for probably the first time in his life. *What on earth is this old fossil up to?*

Speechless, Hardy watched as the skinny, white-haired figure advanced to the autopsy table and waved a hand at the astounded little man who ran the mortuary.

'Open it up, my man! ' snapped the professor.

Hawkins, the attendant, looked from one doctor to the other. His eyes came back to Hardy and he looked appealingly at the local expert.

'Come on, come on!' said Sir Glanville testily, picking up a scalpel from a nearby tray and waving it at Hawkins.

Hardy's blood pressure was climbing rapidly. He stepped forward to the opposite side of the table. 'I'm afraid that Hawkins doesn't normally do that, Professor. I always prefer to examine everything myself. One can't really get a full picture unless one does it that way.'

The white-haired rajah threw down the scalpel with a clatter.

'I was doing post-mortems when you were in prep school, Hardy!' he snapped.

Hardy suppressed his anger with increasing difficulty.

'Look, I'll assist you, sir. Let me have that knife, Hawkins.'

West looked decidedly put out.

'Always have the sweeper to do this where I come from. Job for servants, not a specialist. Looking at the organs, yes, that's for us. But, good God, do you mean to say that you keep a dog and bark yourself?'

Hardy couldn't think of a civil answer to that, but he looked at the knife in his hand, then suddenly put it down.

'Surely, you'll do an external examination first? This is an asphyxia, as you know. There's more to see outside than in.'

Sir Glanville back-tracked a little and made whoofling noises in his throat. 'Well, yes. I've seen the face … seen the skin, yes. Come back to that later.' He waved a finger at Hardy. 'The organs, that's what matters, Hardy. The microscope is the thing. All true pathology depends on the microscope. The disease is in the cells, eh?'

John Hardy gave up at that point. He caught the eye of Sam Partridge, who was standing near the door, his face an almost laughable mask of incredulity.

Hardy's impeccable manners slipped momentarily, enough for him to roll his eyes upwards at Sam, in a message of despair. For Hardy to do this to a layman, in respect of another doctor, was a measure of the exasperation that boiled within him.

'Well then, cut, if you'll be so good,' snapped the white-haired autocrat.

With steam almost issuing from his ears, Hardy reopened the incision he had made from neck to pubis a few days before. For the next half-hour, he watched with mounting incredulity as the colonial gentleman meticulously searched through every organ and minutely examined every part, taking numerous small pieces into a jar of formaldehyde for microscopic examination. Hardy had naturally taken his own similar tissue samples, but merely a routine selection, as the girl had died of straightforward asphyxia – the microscopic examination was only to confirm the absence of any hidden natural diseases.

But Sir Glanville conducted a minute and completely unnecessary scrutiny of every morsel, though seeming oblivious to the parts that mattered most – those on the outside of the body related to the suffocation and the sexual aspects.

Several times Hardy started to give some diplomatic advice, about what he had found or done at his examination, but before half a word had got past his lips, the old professor had shushed him.

'Mustn't tell me, lad. I'm on the other side, you know … against you.'

At this, Sam Partridge had to go out. He couldn't stand there without bursting into peals of laughter at the expression on Hardy's face. At fifty-five, to be called a 'lad' was bad enough, but the utter arrogance of the old man in blandly informing Hardy of his status in the matter was too much.

John Hardy soon had enough of it. 'I'm afraid that I'll have to leave now, Professor,' he said stiffly. 'I think perhaps you'd better get in touch with Mr Kieller, the coroner, if you want any further information.'

Sir Glanville, intent on dissecting the left adrenal gland, hardly looked up.

'Oh, off, are you? Well, see you in court no doubt.'

Hardy left as decorously as possible. Outside, Sam Partridge opened his mouth to speak to him, but Hardy held up a hand.

'Mr Partridge, please. I'm not in a fit state to be talked to, not even by you. I'm off to find a telephone. I'll see you before long, if I don't have a stroke over this.'

He strode to his nearby Range Rover and drove slowly away, fighting the temptation to slam his foot on the accelerator and ram Sir Glanville's hired Daimler slap in the middle.

Hardy drove home, trying to force himself back into a normal frame of mind, but making a poor job of it. He rarely lost his temper, but the high-handed arrogance of Sir Glanville West had for once got the better of him.

When he reached his study, he immediately dialled the University and asked for the Dean of Medicine. Perhaps James Donnington might have some excuse, maybe even know of some mental condition that years in the Indian sun had brought upon the old professor.

'James, John Hardy here. Have you a moment to talk?'

'Certainly. But I thought you were due to be with my old friend Philip this afternoon?'

Hardy gripped the telephone as if it were Glanville West's scrawny throat.

'James, where on earth did that gentleman come from? I've never met such an overbearing man in my life. And, even worse, he doesn't know what he's doing professionally.'

To his surprise, Donnington's voice was noticeably cold when he replied.

'My dear John, I've known him for years. He's a brilliant man. Wasted in India, but he wouldn't come home. I'm sure you must be mistaken.'

'James, I've been in this situation of having a second opinion thrust upon my cases many scores of times, but I've never met with such rudeness before. And rude not only to me, but to the mortuary assistant, which is worse. And even to a senior police officer, who this friend of yours completely ignored. Is the man in full possession of his faculties?'

There was a pause. Hardy could only hear the faint crackling of the telephone connection. Then Donnington spoke again.

'John, I don't like this attitude at all. Just because the man has been set to challenge your professional opinion, is no reason to take exception to him personally.'

Hardy almost had a fit. 'James, that's grossly unfair. You've known me too long to believe an idiotic thing like that. I tell you, this Sir whatever his name is, is utterly unsuitable for a forensic case. He might have been a brilliant histologist but, dammit, he didn't even look at the external appearances and he wouldn't accept any account of the original autopsy. He's taking his fee under false pretences!'

This time it was Donnington's turn to shout down the telephone.

'John, please. Philip has been a friend of mine for many years. I recommended him to Saul Bannerman, so if you accuse him of incompetence, you also call my judgment into question.'

'James, for heaven's sake ...' began Hardy, but the man at the other end kept on talking.

'This professional paranoia is quite unlike you, John. It is quite unjustified for you to launch a personal attack on him, because you fear some challenge to your reputation. I'm sorry to have to say this, John, but you haven't been the same man since you returned. I know that you have had a most grievous experience, but I would hate to think that it had warped your previous impartiality. You are acting for the prosecution, I know, but God forbid that you might have developed some vendetta against every man accused of a killing, because of what happened last summer.'

Hardy was speechless. Had everyone gone mad? James Donnington, an acquaintance, if not perhaps a close friend, for many years, was accusing him of having his judgement warped because of what had happened to Jo!

'James, listen to me,' he said urgently, 'I tell you that this Indian fellow is quite unsuited to the task he's been given. That's all. I even take back my remarks about his insufferable rudeness, if that would satisfy you. But he's just not the man for the job.'

Donnington's voice was like splinters of ice across the line. 'John, I don't think this conversation should be pursued.'

Hardy was completely without words now. He muttered a goodbye and put the phone down.

A cold wave seemed to travel through him as he stood alone in the silent house, almost unable to comprehend the events of the afternoon. Though he was outwardly a resilient person, he was very vulnerable to any personal conflicts. Embarrassment and even shame pursued the outrage and sense of injustice that he felt. It made him almost tremble with the surge of emotions that racked him as he stared at the telephone, the innocent carrier of such troubles.

Looking back on it later, Hardy recognised that it was in that moment, standing alone in his study, that he decided to leave Warwick and start afresh elsewhere.

Chapter Six

The speaker was incredibly boring and Hardy amused himself by turning the numbered dial on the arm of his seat to Channel Four, which gave him the same speech in French. He spent the next five minutes admiringly listening to the translator's efforts to put the poor German of the Bulgarian speaker into something that could be recognised in Paris or Lyon.

It was four weeks after the second autopsy on Penny Vincent. The decision that Hardy had made that day in his study had been set in motion and he expected to be leaving Warwick within the next two months. In the meantime, he had accepted an invitation to attend an International Conference in Munich, being glad of the chance to spend a week out of the now distasteful environment of his own town. Since that exchange of words on the telephone, he and James Donnington had discreetly avoided each other, except on necessary university business. No further mention had been made of Sir Glanville West and his nonsense. Hardy had heard no more of the old gentleman, though it was early days yet in the development of the case of Monty Lever.

The conference in Germany was right up John Hardy's street, being devoted to the question of the identity of individuals. This was a very large field and all manner of questions were to be debated and papers read by research workers from many countries. Hardy's main interest was naturally his hobby horse of the identification of skeletons, but others attending were primarily concerned with the identification of mass casualties, such as air crashes, train accidents, fires in hotels and even catastrophes such as mining disasters and earthquakes.

There were a number of British doctors and scientists present, with a contingent from the Royal Air Force Medical Branch, who were foremost amongst the world's experts on aircraft crashes.

One of these, a doctor he had known for years, sat next to him, as they listened with despair to the stumbling words of the Bulgarian.

'Poor devil is doing his best, but I feel sorry for the translator,' murmured Brian Loftus. He was listening to Channel Two, the English translation. Though he was stationed at an RAF hospital in Dusseldorf, his German was not good enough to pick up the strangled phrases of the man on the rostrum. The Bulgarian was talking about a method of identification using the lobe pattern of the ear, but to the restless audience in the hall, it sounded more like a leg-pull or black magic.

Another five minutes was enough for Hardy.

'What about a cup of coffee?' he hissed at Loftus and, with a ready nod, the wing commander followed him into the steady trickle of delegates who also thought that a cigarette or a coffee was better value at ten thirty in the morning than a Balkan dissertation about earlobes.

'Nice place, this. Nothing to touch it in Britain,' said Brian, as they walked down the thickly carpeted corridor to the cafeteria. The Congress was being held in a special conference centre belonging to the University of Munich. It was in the Leopoldstrasse, in the rather Bohemian area of Schwabing. With several large halls, two with full facilities for simultaneous translation into four languages, the place was a model of what can be done when sufficient money and enterprise is available.

Hardy bought two filter coffees at the counter and took them across to a table which Brian Loftus had managed to obtain in the rapidly filling cafe. He nodded to a number of acquaintances on the way, old and new friends from places as far apart as Sydney and San Francisco.

He set the coffees down and sank with a sigh of relief opposite Brian Loftus. The Air Force expert was a middle-aged man who had the comfortable, rounded look of a stockbroker rather than a specialist on fire injuries and the identification of burnt bodies.

'Usual mix of papers in these meetings – like the curate's egg – good in parts! ' said Loftus cheerily.

Hardy nodded, stirring some sugar into the dark strength of his coffee.

'Thursday is the main attraction for me – the section on skeletal identification. But a lot of the other material is most useful, except for people like our friend back there.' He gestured in the direction of the Bulgarian.

'Nice to meet you again, John. It must be three or four years since we were on that Boeing crash together.'

The wing commander suddenly remembered and his face became grave. 'I heard about your wife. I'm so sorry, John. How are things going with you now?'

Hardy stared into his cup. 'Not too well, Brian, to tell you the truth. I haven't had the same feeling for Warwick since it happened. And there have been some other things that make me yearn for a change.'

'A change. You're leaving?'

Hardy nodded. 'I've decided to pack up and move to the Thames Valley. Go into part-time medico-legal practice there. It will be a complete break with the past. I'll have more opportunity to choose what I want to do.'

Loftus stared across at the compact, self-possessed man opposite. He had thought that he was a fixture in Warwick for the rest of his life.

'Bit of an upheaval for you, John, at your time of life. I don't mean that you're senile or anything but, by our age, most of us have carved out a niche for ourselves and stick in it until we retire. I know I'm in the "Raff" but, when I finish in two years, I've got a consultant post in civilian life already lined up for me.'

Hardy turned up his hands in an almost continental gesture.

'This is the best thing for me, Brian. I've been very lucky, actually. Vinton College at Oxford have offered me a personal Chair in Legal Medicine ... a bit of sinecure, I know, as I'll only be there about one afternoon a week, but it's a foothold in the University. I've also been awarded a research grant from the University Department of Archaeology to do a five-year study on bone dating, so that will take care of the salary of a technician and maybe even a secretary. And on top of that, the Inner London coroner has promised me some routine coroner's post-mortem work a few days a week. So with one thing and the other, I'll be able to keep the wolf from the door and still have time to take on private work.'

'Sounds the ideal set-up,' admitted the wing commander. 'When does all this start?'

'I'm in the process of looking for a place to live. Somewhere between London and Reading would be nice, easy to get into town and out to Oxford. I need room for a laboratory, so it might take me some time to find a suitable house. Then I've got to sell up in Warwick, so I can't see me moving for a couple of months at the earliest.'

'Well, best of luck. You deserve it, John.' He looked at his watch. 'There's that round table discussion on tissue typing in identification in Room Six at eleven o'clock. Are you coming?'

Hardy shook his head. 'I think not, Brian. I want to hear a couple of papers on frontal sinus identification by X-ray. It's in Room One.'

They stood up and moved to the door.

'Where are you staying?' Hardy asked.

'The Hotel Keller on Amalienstrasse. Small, but quite nice.'

'We must have dinner, Brian. Are you free this evening?'

'Sure. That would be marvellous.'

'I'll give you a ring about six. I'm staying at the Berlin, just off the Odeonsplatz.'

They left to go to their respective meetings and for the next two hours, Hardy was immersed in technical details of the frontal sinuses, the air pockets in the skull, situated behind the forehead. Every person has a different shape to these sinuses, so individual that they were like fingerprints. No two persons in the world had so far been found to have identical frontal sinuses.

The papers were in English or German – good German this time, so Hardy had no need of the headphones. He spoke both French and German fluently and often thanked his luck in having good teachers in school, though his years in the Army Medical Corps had given him plenty of opportunity to practise his German in the years after the war.

Just before one o'clock, the session broke up and he wandered off to the bar for a pre-lunch drink. He was not a great beer drinker, preferring wine, but when in Munich it would have been madness not to have taken the opportunity to drink the best light beer in the world.

He stood drinking a half litre of Löwenbräu, chatting to some Belgian pathologists that he knew well. In the compact world of forensic medicine, space and distance were annihilated and one's friends could be from the furthest corners of the globe. In fact, he saw some of them much more often than he saw colleagues from some places in Britain, who rarely attended conferences with the assiduity of the foreign experts.

After lunch, in the excellent restaurant attached to the Congress Hall, Hardy felt like a short walk to blow off the centrally-heated torpor of the building.

He set out for the Englischer Garten, a large park

between the Leopoldstrasse and the River Isar that was the backbone of Munich.

The weather was sharp and he walked quickly, revelling in the immaculately clean streets of that fascinating city.

His feet carried him down the Martiusstrasse, through the Garten as far as the well-known landmark of the Chinese Tower, a pagoda-like structure at the corner of the park.

Then his watch told him it was getting late, so rather reluctantly he turned back, promising himself a longer walk the next day and a visit to the Haus der Kunst, the great art gallery at the other end of the park on Prinzregentstrasse.

As he walked into the foyer of the Congress Hall, he passed the long counter where smartly uniformed girls ran the complicated administration of the conference. Here he had registered and been issued with his plastic briefcase, mass of papers about the meeting, shiny ballpoint and writing pads advertising German pharmaceutical products.

At the end of the counter was a blackboard, used to pass on messages to the people attending the congress. Almost idly, his eyes passed across it, but were at once arrested by the sight of his own name.

DR J. HARDY. URGENT MESSAGE AT REGISTRATION.

Odd, who knew he was here? Hardly anyone in Warwick knew – or cared – where he got to these days.

He went across to the nearest girl, a smart brunette in a green uniform resembling that of an air hostess.

In perfect German, he asked for the message and was handed a folded pink sheet.

PLEASE TELEPHONE 24-35-4426. URGENT was the cryptic message.

He thanked the girl and walked to a row of plastic

bubbles on a nearby wall, each of which concealed a payphone.

He rang the number, expecting to hear a German answering, but to his surprise, a female voice – undoubtedly groomed at Cheltenham or Malvern – informed him that this was the British Consulate.

'This is Dr John Hardy. I had an urgent message, asking me to telephone.'

'Yes, Doctor. Will you hold on one moment, please?'

There were noises of a buzzer calling an extension and the next moment he heard, to his further surprise, the voice of Brian Loftus.

'Good heavens, Brian, what's going on. Have you been arrested?'

His attempts at mild humour were stifled by the serious reply of the normally light-hearted wing commander.

'John, sorry to have troubled you. Look, are you very keen on staying at the meeting this afternoon?'

Mystified, Hardy said that he had intended listening to a few papers, but there was nothing of great interest to him.

'I can't say much on the phone, but would you do me a great favour and help me out. It's a matter of identification, amongst other things, but the real McCoy, not just talking about it.'

Hardy realised that something important was involved and had the sense not to question it any further on the telephone.

'If you think I can help, by all means. What do you want me to do?'

'Thanks, John. I'll tell you all about the problem when we get you here. I'll have a car sent over right away. Should be there in fifteen minutes.'

A quarter of an hour later, a still bemused Hardy was sitting in a large Mercedes, carrying diplomatic plates, riding through the streets of Munich. It was a short drive to the consulate building and very soon Hardy was ushered into an office where Brian Loftus sat with three men in civilian clothes and a group captain in RAF uniform.

There were introductions all round, but the only names that Hardy remembered were Shaddick for the senior Air Force man and Turnbull for the eldest plain-clothes man. The other two, one a German, said very little the whole time.

'It's a matter of the identification and cause of death of a body, John,' began Brian. 'I'll let Mr Turnbull here explain the guts of the affair.'

Turnbull, who looked very like a policeman to Hardy, was a large, solid man with the calm manner and deliberate movements that were so typical of experienced investigators.

'Dr Hardy, you have been most flatteringly vouched for by the wing commander here. I know that you have in the past been involved in both Home Office and Foreign Office cases which required the utmost discretion.'

Hardy inclined his head as an acknowledgment of the graceful compliment.

'We have a situation here which is *also* one which needs discretion and secrecy. As you might have guessed already, I represent the Ministry of Defence in an intelligence capacity.'

He nodded towards the other Englishman.

'My colleague here is a Special Branch officer and our German friend is from the Munich police department.'

'And I'm just a poor bloody airman who happens to run a small RAF unit quartered in the German military air base outside the city,' added the group captain.

Turnbull took up the story again.

'In a nutshell, Doctor Hardy, a dead man was found floating in the River Isar this morning. Papers on the body indicate that he was a British research engineer named Colin Monks. It now becomes vital to us – indeed, a matter of national security – to make absolutely sure that the body is that of Monks and, if so, was he killed or did he take his own life?'

There was a silence while Hardy thought this through.

'Can I ask why this is so important? I'll not take the slightest offence if you tell me it's none of my business.'

Turnbull gave a lazy smile. 'Probably I shouldn't tell you, but I will. I think that if you're good enough to help us, you're entitled to know why you're doing it.'

He paused while there was a tap on the door and a servant of the Consulate brought in a large tray of tea. When he had left, Turnbull carried on, as Loftus quietly handed round the cups.

'Colin Monks was an ex-RAF scientific officer. Though he became a civilian four years ago, he continued to work at a top-security missile research establishment, at Aberporth on the coast of West Wales. He had been there for some years and in fact been in on the development and trials of the Seaslug missile.'

Turnbull paused to sip his tea.

'Six weeks ago, he vanished. Disappeared off the face of the earth, not a trace of him turned up anywhere. Naturally, we were as worried as hell, because although not a great deal is going on at Aberporth these days, he had a lot of information tucked away in his head.

'We didn't know if he had "done a Philby" on us – either defected or even just gone home after twenty years' service as a Soviet agent. The other possibility was that he was abducted. Snatched from under our noses.'

He paused again to drink from his cup, leaving Hardy in suspense.

'Then, early today, a body was found in the river on the outskirts of Munich, very decomposed and unrecognisable. To the police it was just another "drowner", but they found a British passport in the pocket. It was sodden but readable and when they saw it was in the name of Colin Monks, they naturally contacted the British Consulate here.'

'Still without any suspicion, naturally,' put in the quiet Special Branch man, who reminded Hardy of Detective Inspector Williams, back in Norton Heath.

'The Consulate had his name in a general panic signal that we sent all over the world six weeks ago. They telexed the Foreign Office. I was having my breakfast in Surbiton at eight o'clock this morning – at ten, I was on an RAF jet along with my friend here.'

Brian Loftus came back into the conversation.

'I haven't seen the body yet, John, but the problem is one of making a cast-iron identification and then deciding whether he jumped or whether he was pushed!'

'It makes all the difference to the security side,' explained Turnbull. 'If he was snatched, has he told all he knows? He might even have been tortured, I suppose; that would be vital to learn. If he went of his own free will, has he been tumbled by the opposition and killed? Or has he died by his own actions accidentally, or even committed suicide, perhaps in remorse for having done a bunk? There are so many unknowns, but we must know as much as we can, so that we can at least estimate our losses.'

The intelligence man stood up and walked to the window, where he swung around to face them.

'It may not even be Monks! Either he or the other side may have done a substitution to make us think he's dead, while in fact he's sitting in Moscow or Baikonur, drawing them plans of our antiquated missiles.'

Hardy, utterly intrigued by things he had only read about in the fictional pages of Le Carré and Deighton, was only too pleased to help. If nothing else, it completely banished thoughts of Warwick, Lever and Donnington, which even the Munich congress had not entirely obliterated.

They all went in the huge Mercedes out on the peripheral road and then along part of the autobahn, in the direction of Dachau and from there to an air base some miles north.

Inside the perimeter, they drove to the group of buildings in front of which fluttered .the blue RAF ensign. Hardy never discovered what function the place played, but that was none of his business.

They walked through the front part of the building, out through a rear door and into a smaller unit which contained a number of rooms off a central corridor. Hardy saw RAF technicians and WRAF personnel through open doors, either sitting at typewriters or handling electronic equipment on workbenches.

'After six weeks, we had to put him well out of the way, I'm afraid,' said the group captain, as they crossed yet another open area and entered a small, flat-roofed building. 'This used to be an ammunition store, but it came in handy for a mortuary.'

He opened the door and immediately Hardy's nostrils were filled with the familiar stench of putrefaction.

The German detective hung back with the Special Branch man, reluctant to go inside. They had already seen the body and felt disinclined to go in again until really necessary.

Hardy and Loftus went inside, followed less willingly by Shaddick and Turnbull.

The room was quite bare, white painted brickwork forming the walls. There was no window, as would be natural in an explosives store, but two powerful strip lights in the ceiling threw a brilliant glare down on to a decomposed body lying on a metal tray propped on trestles in the centre of the room.

The body was nothing out of the ordinary to Hardy and his eyes moved immediately to a more unusual sight. Sitting at ease on a folding chair near the body, was a uniformed RAF staff sergeant, nonchalantly reading a newspaper. Apart from the rotting corpse, he and his chair were the only objects in the cell-like room and Hardy was reminded of some avant-garde stage set.

The sergeant had his back to the door and it was several seconds before he realised that someone had entered. He looked over his shoulder and jumped up when he saw the imposing uniform of a group captain. He stood stiffly to attention alongside his chair, his newspaper at the slope.

'All right, Staff, stand easy,' said Shaddick.

He turned to the other pair.

'I thought we had better keep an eye on the body until it was dealt with. None of my ordinary men were all that keen on holding the hand of a thing like that,' – he looked at the wreckage of the body with distaste – 'but thankfully we had Price in the unit, who doesn't seem to mind. Do you, Price?'

Price grinned impishly. 'Not a bit, sir. A pleasure, sir.'

Somehow he managed to inject just the slightest sarcasm into the words, without letting anything drop that could be turned against him. Hardy felt that here was a cunning professional soldier, who had learned all the tricks the hard way. Price was quite a young man, probably in his late twenties. Though every item of his uniform was correct, somehow the whole did not 'gel' together. There was a vague hint of general bloody-mindedness about the man that was at variance with his rank of staff sergeant. He had a full face, with bright eyes and Hardy, who from the first was intrigued by the man, felt that here was someone who had an IQ that would have fitted a university professor, but who had the ethics of a second-hand car salesman.

'Price has strong medical connections,' went on the Group Captain. 'He's a Class One Medical Laboratory Technician by trade … umpteen years' service in, eh, Price?'

'Quite a few, sir,' said Price.

Again there was the slightest pause before he answered, that indicated that he did things on his own terms, at least to the limit with which he could get away with it.

'He was here on some other technical duty,' went on Shaddick with deliberate vagueness. 'Actually, you're just about finished with the Force, Price, isn't that right?'

'Sir, yes. My terminal leave starts on Saturday.'

'No hope of getting you to sign on for another seven, eh?'

'Not this time, no, sir.' There was a finality in his tone that suggested that last time he had done the wrong thing.

Turnbull came reluctantly from near the door where the smell was least.

'I suppose we should think ourselves lucky, having Wing Commander Loftus and Doctor Hardy in Munich at a time like this. Otherwise we might have had to ship him home by air and that creates all sorts of problems with the German authorities. As it is they've been very good in releasing the case to our military custody, instead of handling it themselves.'

'That's why our German police colleague is here – at least, he's outside. He's here to square things from the civil authority point of view.'

Hardy and Loftus approached the trestles and looked at the ruined man lying there. The head was partly reduced to a skull and the bones of the hands and legs were exposed in places through the greyish, liquefying skin. There was a jacket on the body, with remnants of shirt and underclothes, but most of the trousers had been torn away, presumably by friction and impact with the rocks of the river bed.

'All the German police did was look in his pockets,' said Turnbull. 'As soon as they found his passport, they stopped.'

Loftus looked at Hardy. 'This is more in your line than it is mine. I'm an identification boffin, I know, but mainly of burnt and smashed air crash victims. I leave it to you to come up with the ideas, if you're willing to help.'

Hardy nodded. This was a challenge mixed with rather exotic circumstances – something he couldn't resist.

'I'd be delighted to do all I can. Now, what about the actual mechanics of the job?'

Loftus looked at Shaddick. 'What can we get laid on, sir?'

The group captain waved a hand round the ammunition store.

'Can we manage here, do you think? This is a security operation; we would very much prefer not to have to hawk the body round the countryside to some hospital. The fewer people who know about this the better, in case our eastern bloc chums haven't had wind of it yet.'

'The place is adequate, if you don't mind it smelling for the next six months,' replied John Hardy. 'But we'd need some facilities. Protective clothing, instruments, maybe photography and perhaps some laboratory aids. Is that at all possible?'

Shaddick looked, not at the RAF doctor, but at the staff sergeant.

'Price? Can do?'

The lean-faced technician gave a crooked grin.

'All laid on already, sir. I phoned the Raff hospital at Bielefeld this morning. Spoke to some of my contacts, sir.'

'You mean the stuff can be flown down from there?'

'Can be, sir? It's here already, outside, in a box.'

The senior officer's face was a picture as he contemplated the 'old boy network' that allowed a crafty regular NCO to get Ministry of Defence supplies flown around Europe at a couple of hours' notice without any reference to 'official channels'.

But wisely he said nothing and the look in Price's eye showed that he savoured his triumph over red tape and bull.

Within a few minutes, Hardy and Loftus were wearing operating gowns, caps and boots, with lightweight plastic aprons and rubber gloves to keep off the worst of the offensiveness from the body.

Like magic, Price had produced buckets, a roll of surgical instruments, specimen bottles and other paraphernalia which showed the depth of both his technical knowledge and his anticipation of general requirements. Hardy's heart warmed to him, as he compared him with some of the technical help that he knew at home.

When he had laid out all his treasures, Price vanished outside and soon returned with a Polaroid camera and flashgun. He stood waiting to take any photographs that were needed. The Special Branch man came back with him.

'The first thing we need to know, of course, is all possible details about Colin Monks,' said Hardy.

Turnbull produced a brown folder from under his arm, and pulled out a bundle of papers.

'We've brought everything from his Service records and some other data from his security clearances. Not all that much on the physical side, but it's all we've got.'

Hardy went up to the body and ran a critical eye along its length.

'No doubt about the sex, so we want to know height, age and anything that might give a lead to personal identity.'

'And the cause of death, if humanly possible. Or at least, did he fall or was he pushed, in your opinion,' added Brian Loftus.

Hardy walked around to the other side of the metal tray. The two doctors stood there facing each other. Shaddick thought that they looked like a pair of vultures sizing up their prey.

'The height? Have we a record of Monk's height?'

asked Hardy.

As Shaddick shuffled the papers, Price stepped forward from his position at the foot of the trestles and offered Hardy a roll-up metal tape-measure.

Again, the pathologist was impressed by the anticipation the man had of the wishes of others.

'Five feet ten, according to his documents,' said the senior RAF man.

Price held the end of the tape while Hardy pulled the other end out. With the six-foot measure out to its full length, the distance from the heel to the top of the bare skull was five feet, eight and a half inches.

'That's about right for him,' observed Loftus.

Shaddick stared at him. 'It's almost two inches short,' he objected.

Hardy shook his head. 'We have to allow for the thickness of the scalp, say half an inch. Then the loss of tension in the discs of the spine can account for another inch, especially in a body in such a poor state as this.'

Brian Loftus was prodding about in the almost fleshless jaws.

'No natural teeth, damn it. Remains of bare gums. The jaws have shrunk down; he must have had a total dental extraction quite a time ago.'

'And presumably there were no dentures found near the body?' asked Hardy.

The Special Branch shook his head. 'Nothing else, sir. The river is quite fast-flowing where he was found. The body had been caught up on a tree trunk jammed in the middle of a shoal, but it may have come miles from where it went into the water originally. Anything like teeth or the rest of his clothes could be scattered over fifty miles.'

Hardy asked Price to take some photographs of the body and for the next few minutes, the flash of the sergeant's Polaroid camera lit up the old ammunition store.

When he had finished and the instant prints had been

approved, he stood back again while the pathologists carried on with the next stage. There was no record of whether the missing Colin Monks had possessed false teeth, but the Special Branch man had gone out to phone London to see if the information could be obtained rapidly.

'Those records seem particularly unhelpful,' observed Loftus, as they looked over Shaddick's shoulder at the folder. 'Brown hair … the body has none. Brown eyes … empty eye sockets.'

The group captain grunted as he turned over the pages of the service record. 'We've also got his fingerprints – but the fingers here are bony stumps.'

Hardy pointed with a rubber-clad forefinger at something on the page. 'There's the blood group. A Rhesus-positive. One of the most common you can get. But it's better than nothing.'

He turned to Price, who was waiting impassively across the room.

'Staff Sergeant, can you put up a blood group?'

'Sir, yes, sir. If I have the facilities.'

Hardy nodded, more impressed than ever with the directness of the man.

'And have you got them … or can you get them?'

'There's a small hospital attached to this base, sir. I'm sure that if the group captain could arrange for me to use their laboratory, the Germans would let me use their stuff.'

Shaddick nodded. 'I'll have a word with the commander here. I know him quite well. Perhaps the German technicians would actually do the test.'

Turnbull said 'I'd rather keep it all in British hands, if possible. If they can't give facilities to Price here, then we could fly it to the British zone up north or even back to UK.'

'I'll see about it when we've done here,' promised Shaddick.

As the two gowned and booted figures began probing

and delving into the body, Price again hovered about, handing instruments, taking samples of tissue and fluid, generally proving himself useful.

The tattered remnants of clothing were taken off and placed in plastic bags. Turnbull promised that they would be flown back to London that evening, to be matched as best as possible with any clothes that Monks had possessed. The man was a bachelor and lived alone in the Welsh seaside village that housed the rocket research station.

'There was nothing else in the pockets or on the labels to help,' reported the Special Branch man, who had returned from his phone call by this stage. 'Not even enough to tell whether the jacket was British. The passport was in a buttoned pocket inside the jacket.'

Hardy had finished a detailed external examination of the body by now. 'Nothing at all to indicate violence before death,' he said. 'Even though the state of the chap is so bad, we can at least tell that he wasn't shot, stabbed or beaten to death.'

Loftus let Hardy make the running and merely stood by now to help when asked, as this type of examination was not really in his field. As the Warwick pathologist began to open the body and remove the organs, Shaddick and Turnbull were going through the papers from London all over again, to see if there was anything they had missed the first time.

'I suppose this is no use, Doc?' asked Turnbull. 'Two years ago, Monks had a slight accident in one of the workshops at the rocket base. It says that an electronic unit weighing about seven pounds slipped out of a casing and struck him on the head. He was knocked out for a moment and taken to hospital, but was not kept in. It's just an accident report, not a medical report. Monks was off work for four days, that's all.'

Hardy put down his knife and turned round. 'Head

injury and concussion. That could be just the thing we want to clinch it, if we're lucky.'

Loftus stared at him. 'There's no mark on the skull. You'd hardly expect it with such a trivial injury.'

Hardy shook his head. 'I didn't mean the injury itself. I wondered if Monks had an X-ray of his skull when he was taken to hospital. It's the usual thing after someone gets concussed.'

Loftus whistled. 'Yes ... that really would clinch it. Can we find out, Mr Turnbull. Get an urgent message off to wherever he was taken after the accident.'

The Special Branch man again hurried off to the telephone, while Hardy explained to Turnbull and Shaddick how the X-ray could help.

'The shape of the skull can be matched up against an X-ray of this chap here. Oddly enough, there was a paper read at this conference today about the use of skull X-rays in identification.'

'The frontal sinuses are the best bet,' added Brian Loftus. 'The air cells between the eyebrows are always different in every person. If we get a match, we're home and dry.'

As the examination went on, Hardy confirmed that there was no sign of physical violence. 'All this damage to the head and limbs is post-mortem. Partly decomposition, partly from injury against objects in the river. Internally, he's not too badly putrefied. How long since he was last seen alive?'

'About six weeks.'

'I'd guess he's been in the water at least four of those weeks, but as it's been a fairly cold autumn, he's not gone off too badly. Let's have a look at this stomach ... again, it's still intact, you see.'

Turnbull did see, though he would have preferred not to. Then Hardy and Loftus both made sudden exclamations as Hardy opened the stomach into a small bowl that Price handed to him.

'Something amiss here!' snapped Hardy.

Shaddick and Turnbull watched as a lumpy white mass fell into the bowl.

'What on earth is that?'

'A mass of powder … looks like dissolved tablets. Yes, there's still one or two almost intact in the middle of it. A small handful of the stuff.'

Loftus prodded the contents of the bowl with the handle of a scalpel.

'White tablets. Could be a hundred things, but they're about the size of aspirin.'

John Hardy nodded. 'Aspirin is quite a good bet, actually. The stomach lining is too far decomposed to show much, unfortunately. If it was fresher, we might see some erosions from the stuff.'

Price stepped forward. 'Excuse me, sir. What about a ferric chloride test?'

Hardy looked up at him, his admiration going up another notch.

'Have you got some?'

'Ten minutes and I'll scrounge some from the German lab, sir.'

He vanished through the door without further ado.

Hardy stared after him. 'Remarkable chap, that. I'd never expect to find an Air Force NCO in a place like this, who knew so much about general laboratory work.'

Loftus and Shaddick grinned at each other. 'Good advertisement for the Regular Forces, eh,' said Shaddick. 'Our chaps are on the ball as much as you civvies!'

Hardy smiled and said 'I'll see if I can stump him when he comes back with something a bit more obscure. We want to know if this fellow drowned or whether he was thrown in after he was dead.'

Turnbull stared at Hardy. 'You can't possibly tell after all this time, surely?'

Hardy shrugged. 'Maybe, maybe not. But we'll have a try, eh, Brian?'

Loftus thought for a moment then light dawned in his face. 'Ah, yes, the diatom technique. Never had much luck with it myself, but you never know.'

When Price came back, sauntering in with ill-concealed complacency at having 'won' some ferric chloride, Hardy was ready for him.

'Well done, Staff Sergeant. Now do you think you could arrange some nitric acid, a centrifuge and a microscope through your "diplomatic channels"?'

By late morning on the following day, the whole case was virtually sewn up. The previous evening Hardy had gone back to his hotel after the post-mortem and later had the promised dinner with Brian Loftus. No news had come back from Britain by then, but was promised by the following morning.

When that morning came, John Hardy was quite happy to leave the conference once more and accompany his wing commander friend back to the German air base.

Shaddick had been as good as his word and had arranged with the base commander to have the use of a small side room in the laboratory attached to the camp hospital.

Price had moved in early and had everything set up with his usual laconic efficiency, by the time the two doctors arrived.

'I've set up a blood grouping rack, sir,' he announced, leaning ever so slightly against the edge of the bench to indicate his lack of awe at having such senior medical colleagues. 'Should be readable in about half an hour.'

Hardy nodded and looked with approval at the apparatus laid neatly on the bench under the window.

'How's that tissue looking, the stuff we put in acid overnight?'

Price went to a fume cupboard in the corner, a sort of mini-greenhouse designed to keep smelly or harmful vapours from leaking into the room. He slid up the glass front and took out a tray of small glass jars.

'They've been in a water bath since seven o'clock this morning. I've let them cool down and they're ready for neutralising.'

Hardy took the jars and set them in a row on the main bench. They were labelled 'lung', 'liver', 'kidney' and 'bone marrow'.

'Have you ever seen this technique before, Sergeant Price?'

Price tried to look bored, but a glitter in his eye betrayed the fact that he was keen to hear all about it.

'It all depends on whether or not a person drowns or goes into the water already dead,' put in Loftus.

'And whether there are diatoms in the water,' added Hardy.

Price looked from one to the other. 'Diatoms are those little algae things, aren't they. We used to use them for testing the accuracy of microscope lenses.'

'That's it. They are in ponds and rivers and a different sort in the sea. When someone drowns, they get sucked into the lungs and penetrate into the bloodstream, so if the heart was beating, they get carried round the body to places like the kidney and bone marrow.'

Price nodded his quick understanding. 'And if the chap is dead, they don't.'

Hardy tapped the little jars.

'Right. They're microscopic plants with a silica shell, which resists nitric acid. So we take bits of kidney and bone marrow or whatever and dissolve it in acid. All the tissue is destroyed, but the diatoms survive.'

Price took the jars and carefully tipped each one into a beaker, the brown fumes of the acid curling up above the brim.

'You said neutralise by diluting and washing three times, sir.'

'That's it. Centrifuge each time, to make sure we don't lose any solid. After the third time, we have a look under the mike.'

For the next fifteen minutes, Hardy watched Price expertly adding distilled water and spinning down the fluids in an electric centrifuge, a kind of washing machine contraption that spun the bottles at many thousands of revolutions a minute.

He saw again that the Air Force technician worked with a steady, sure hand, needing no further prompting as to how to go about it.

Eventually, Price handed him four small slips of glass, each carrying a drop of the final fluid.

'A nice microscope over there, sir. A new Zeiss. The German medical corps must be flush to afford mikes like that.'

Hardy sat down on a swivel stool and switched on the light under the instrument.

'Let's have a look at the lung first. If there's no diatoms in that, we've been wasting our time, as it means that there's none in the Isar.'

He adjusted the eye pieces and stared down the microscope, gently turning the focussing and traversing knobs as he watched.

'Good … quite a few there. I was afraid that perhaps there might not be any, due to pollution or the autumn weather coming on.'

'Does that mean he *did* drown, sir?' asked Price, his curiosity getting the better of his assumed indifference.

'No, not in the lungs. Even a dead body can allow water down that far. It's the other organs that count, as the heart must be beating to push the diatoms from the lung to more distant parts of the body.'

He picked up the slide of the bone marrow extract and

silently stared at it with a magnification of five hundred.

The other two stood behind him expectantly.

Suddenly he shifted his head aside. 'Have a look,' he invited.

Loftus motioned Price to look first.

'Yeah. There they are! That's quite a test, sir.'

Price grinned at Hardy, a mixture of pride and pleasure at having brought it off, like a cook with her first Christmas pudding.

Hardy warmed to the man, there was something about Price that struck a sympathetic chord in him.

Loftus was looking now.

'There's no doubt about it, is there? I've only tried a couple of times myself and never got it to work.'

Hardy went back to the eyepieces and talked from there. 'There are a lot of them. Bone marrow is the best place. If you can ensure that the technique is correct, as we did yesterday, seeing as many as this is cast-iron evidence. One or two might be a spurious result, but I'll bet they are in kidney and liver as well.'

They were, and the two pathologists were quite happy about telling Turnbull that the man – whoever he was – had died of drowning.

'And the aspirin, sir. That ferric chloride test on the stomach and the bladder was confirmed by the German laboratory on the blood.'

Price, by his mysterious means of getting anything done on his private scrounging system, had confirmed that the white mass in the stomach of the dead man was indeed aspirin.

'All adds up to suicide, John,' said Brian Loftus. 'Even I know that suicides often take out a double insurance against failure by using two means to kill themselves. Poison and drowning in this case.'

Hardy agreed. 'But we still have to make sure who the chap really is, now.' He turned to Price. 'Is that group ready to read, do you think?'

A few minutes later, Price had confirmed that the blood group of the body was A Rhesus positive. Even though the blood of the decayed man was in a bad state, it was still relatively easy to get a reliable answer and again Hardy was grateful for having such a confident technician as Price to carry out the tests.

'A very common group, the second commonest there is. But it all adds up,' he commented, as they waited for the next stage. It soon came, as the internal telephone summoned them over to the small X-ray unit of the German hospital, where Shaddick and Turnbull were waiting.

Shaddick waved two very large, flat envelopes at them as they came in.

'Everything you asked for, Doctor,' he said. 'The hospital in Carmarthen produced the X-rays from Monks' accident. We had them flown out overnight. No expense spared on a job like this!'

Hardy took the envelope and pointed to the other one.

'Those are the ones taken here, I presume?'

'Yes, our faithful Staff Sergeant Price organised that last evening, after you'd gone. He helped one of the German radiography technicians to push a portable X-ray set over to the improvised mortuary.'

He handed across the second envelope and put his hands together in front of his chest, as if in prayer.

'Do your best for us, Doc. What d'you say to that, Mr Turnbull?'

The Intelligence Officer grinned rather weakly. Although he had 'kept his cool' through all this, there was a real panic going on back in Whitehall.

'As long as we know, one way or the other. Is this really Monks, or have some cunning security men on the "other side" tried to plant a body on us, with Monks' passport deliberately left on him?'

Hardy handed the two envelopes to Brian Loftus.

'I think you should take first look, Brian. You're the Air Force man here and frontal sinuses are more your province than mine.'

Hardy was being diplomatic and courteous, more than strictly accurate, but Loftus went to a large perspex screen set into the wall of the office and pressed a switch. There was a flicker, then the white panels were lit up by strong fluorescent lights behind them.

He opened the first envelope and slid out some big black negative films.

'These are the hospital X-rays of Monks, from Wales,' he said as he jerked the films under holding clips at the tops of the panel. 'And these are our client over in the ammunition room.'

He pushed up a second set of X-rays alongside the first two. There was a long silence as the men looked at them. Price hovered in the background, peering over Hardy's shoulder.

'Well? What's the verdict?' snapped Turnbull, his voice betraying the anxiety hidden under his calm exterior.

There was another pregnant silence, then Hardy slowly turned to the RAF medical man.

'What d'you think, Brian?'

'Looks identical to me, John. Both anterior-posterior and the lateral views seem absolutely the same.'

As Turnbull let out a relieved hiss of breath, Loftus took one of the films, a picture of the head viewed from the front and slid it under the clips of the other similar view. He adjusted the top sheet of blackened gelatine until it registered exactly with the one underneath.

'Superimposes exactly! The sinus pattern is dead on.'

Hardy nodded and touched other parts of the film with the end of a pen. 'So do the tip of the chin, the eye sockets and the cheekbones. It must be the same chap.'

Shaddick clapped his hands: 'You're quite certain? Not

going to have any second thoughts?'

Loftus clapped Hardy on the back. 'We're not going to have second thoughts, are we, John? But we're going to have a nice long beer in the mess. Job's over, another pair of satisfied customers.'

The tension had gone and, chattering with the sudden relaxation, they made their way out of the German medical department.

Turnbull went off to find a telephone, promising to see them back in the British Officers' Mess.

As they walked across the well-kept paths, Price suddenly stopped and saluted.

'I'll be off then, sir. I go this way.'

Rather guiltily, Hardy realised that the Officers' Mess would naturally rule out Price from joining in the celebratory drinks. He walked a few steps away from the other men and held out his hand to Price.

'Staff Sergeant, I've been most impressed by your ability and helpfulness in this affair. I'm more grateful than I can express in words. But thank you very much indeed.'

'That's all right, sir. Just doing my job.'

John Hardy shook his head. 'It was more than that. Some of the people I have to endure do their job too, but it leaves a lot to be desired. Look, didn't you say you were on the point of being demobbed?'

'Next week, sir.'

Hardy looked thoughtful. 'Have you got anything lined up in Civvy Street?'

Price shook his head. He looked rather sad, Hardy thought. *Must be an odd feeling, to be suddenly pitched out into the hard competitive world after so many years in the shelter of the Services.*

He took out his wallet and handed Price his personal card.

'Look, if you're at a loose end for a technical

job … maybe only temporarily, until you get settled, look me up at any time. I can't promise anything, but I've a lot of contacts. And it's possible – not more than that – that I may want someone myself within the next few months.'

For once Price seemed to lose the slightly cynical expression that he usually wore. He bowed his head slightly.

'Thanks a lot, sir. I may just take you up on that.'

He saluted again and swinging round, walked away towards the Sergeants' Mess without looking back.

Hardy caught up with Brian Loftus just before they reached the British section.

'Odd fellow, that staff sergeant. But dammit, he's a fine technician. I'd like to think I haven't seen the last of him.'

Chapter Seven

The Munich affair had been an interesting interlude, but Hardy was brought back to harsh reality as soon as he returned to Warwick. The business of the missing scientist had only occupied a part of two days and the rest of the conference had passed uneventfully.

He flew home to Heathrow on Sunday and by early afternoon was back at home.

Amongst the pile of medical journals, drug advertisements and bills lying on the hall carpet was an official-looking letter. When Hardy turned it over, he saw the familiar words 'Clerk to the Magistrates' printed on the flap. He was used to receiving scores of these every year, but when he opened it, he was surprised to see that it was a Witness Order to appear at Norton Heath Magistrates' Court in a week's time, to give evidence in the case of Regina versus Montague Lever. He was surprised for two reasons – firstly, that the preliminary hearing should have been listed so quickly, for it would be only some six weeks since the death of Penny Vincent. Secondly, the letter made it clear that Hardy was actually required to attend to give evidence, a most unusual thing these days. Since the law was changed back in 1967, the hearing at the Magistrates' Court was almost always a paper exercise, with only lawyers present. The object of this hearing was to commit the case to the Crown Court, where the case would be tried before a judge and jury, when all important witnesses were heard.

Hardy suspected that the reason for the unusual procedure was that the defence were trying to get the case dismissed at the Magistrates' Court, so that it would never be sent for trial.

Next day, he telephoned Detective Chief Superintendent Carrol, to find out what were his feelings about it. Alice confirmed his suspicions.

'The defence obviously reckon they've got a damn good case. And the fact that they want you there means that medical evidence is going to be challenged. You can set your mind on having a pretty good hammering in the witness box, Doc!'

Hardy was never worried about the prospect of a tough time when giving evidence. In fact, he rather relished the cut and thrust between witness and counsel, as long as he had complete faith in the strength of his evidence. It was only on the rare occasions when he felt that he was wandering into the quicksands of uncertainty, that the witness box became an uncomfortable place to stand.

With the prospect of a hard cross-examination ahead, he spent a lot of time that week in going over the material and reports of both the dead girls.

As Lever was only to be charged with the murder of the second girl, Penny Vincent, nothing relating to the first victim would enter into the evidence. Even so, Hardy wanted to have everything at his fingertips from both cases, merely to be on the alert if something unusual cropped up.

He had heard nothing of the aged Professor Glanville West. Moreover, he deliberately kept clear of James Donnington, even to the extent of avoiding the Senior Common Room and the restaurant. Their paths did cross once, in a faculty meeting on the Wednesday, but not a word was mentioned about the case and their conversation was decidedly distant, being confined solely to university matters.

The Lever case was due to start on the next Monday morning, and on the preceding Saturday Hardy decided to spend the day in physical activity. The silence of the house was beginning to get on his nerves again. He found that he was making excuses to himself on every possible occasion to stay out of it as much as possible. Three nights that week he had gone out for a meal, either to a hotel or to friends. Hardy found himself worrying that he might be angling for invitations to dinner parties too often. He hated the thought that he might get the reputation of a professional guest.

He played a round of golf on Saturday morning, had a scratch lunch at the golf club, then promised himself a few hours in his garden in the afternoon.

Since going away on his long cruise, he had lost his regular garden help, who used to come in twice a week. The large garden looked much the worse for wear – autumn leaves were plastered over the lawns and there was a general air of damp neglect that he could stand no longer, especially if he was soon to put it up for sale.

His wellingtons – the same ones that he used for trampling around murder scenes – and some old clothes came out again and, for an hour or so, he found positive enjoyment in raking and brushing. His pulse rate rose and he became slightly out of breath, due to his lack of condition. But the warmth of honest toil, both in his body and in his mind, more than compensated for the effort.

He was scratching sodden leaves off a strip of lawn between two sad-looking rose beds, when he became aware of someone watching him. Looking down the gravel drive to the wide-open iron gates, he saw the figure of a man standing with a bag in his hand. It was quite a long drive and at that distance, Hardy at first failed to recognise the figure. All he saw was a grey raincoat and a rather stylish cap, the sort that one saw on the gentleman farmers and local squires at markets and county shows.

Hardy stood upright, grimacing at a twinge in his back. Leaning on the handle of his rake, he looked back in puzzlement at the man. He knew that face, who the devil was it?

The man seemed to make up his mind and began walking up the drive. As soon as he moved, Hardy recognised the walk. It was Staff Sergeant Price. He looked so different out of the Air Force blue uniform.

'Price! Good heavens, you're the last person I expected to see.'

He stepped over the muddy flower border and stood in the drive, his hand outstretched.

'Sorry to drop in like this, Doctor. But you did say to look you up.'

For once, Price sounded a little unsure of himself, as if he was afraid that Hardy's invitation had been merely a polite insincerity.

But John Hardy was not given to baseless promises.

'Nice to see you, sergeant ... though I shouldn't call you that, I suppose. You'll be a genuine civilian by now, eh?'

Price grinned crookedly and looked down at his raincoat.

'Funny to get rid of the old blue, after all this time.'

Hardy threw his rake down on to the gravel, secretly thankful for an excuse to stop work.

'I was just pining for a cup of tea. Come on in and have one.'

They sat around the kitchen table a few minutes later, crouched over hot cups and some rather tasteless shop cake that Hardy found in a cupboard.

'I should have given you a ring, Doctor. But I had nothing else to do after getting away from the depot on Thursday, so I thought I might as well come up to Warwick as go anywhere else.'

Hardy asked no questions, but understood that Price had no close family and certainly was not married.

'Where are you staying?' he asked.

'I stayed in a big pub in Warwick last night. I felt like getting around England a bit. I've been in Germany for three years and before that I was abroad for quite a time. You know, here and there.'

Even after Hardy got to know Price very well, he still never filled in the details of these indeterminate duties 'here and there'. From some veiled references that Brian Loftus and Shaddick had made in Munich, it was clear that Price's activities in the Air Force were sometimes much more shady than a mere medical technician's.

He stared into his cup, which he rotated restlessly in its saucer. 'You were good enough to mention that you might be able to find something for me to do for a time, Doctor … just until I get settled down, that is,' he added quickly. 'That little bit of forensic work I did for you the other week, well, it appealed to me a lot. I'd like to have a shot at some more, if there was any opening.'

Hardy's mind worked fast. It seemed a coincidence planned by fate that only the previous day, the grant for the bone-dating research had been finally approved by Oxford. Part of the money was earmarked for a laboratory technician – and here was one knocking on his door, one whom Hardy had seen with his own eyes to be unusually proficient.

Hardy tapped his chin gently, a gesture he used when his mental processes were meshing particularly well.

'I might be able to offer you something, Mister Price, but it won't be here, it will be down in the Home Counties.'

Price's face remained impassive, but a little of the gleam went from his eyes.

'Oh. I thought … well, I'd have liked to work for you, if it were possible.'

Hardy nodded. 'It would be for me. I'm going to move in the near future. Packing up here in a few months and shifting lock, stock and barrel to a place between London and Oxford, as I'll be working in both places.'

He went on to explain the whole bone project and after they had finished their tea, he took Price into the laboratory and showed him some of the work that was in progress on the skeletons.

Once again, he was impressed by the instant grasp that Price had about the technical details. He was convinced that this was the right man.

They talked for an hour or two about photography, technology and all manner of laboratory work, until Hardy began to feel hungry.

'Come down to the King's Arms and we'll have a drink and something to eat,' he invited.

Over a meal in the lounge bar, Hardy finally offered Price a trial period of employment at a standard rate of salary, starting at once, as he could begin some of the bone work right away.

'There'll be a lot of packing and moving, to get my equipment down to the south,' warned Hardy. 'Though I've not even bought a house there yet.'

Then the matter of Price's accommodation cropped up. He was content to find a bedsitter in the district, but Hardy – influenced by the thought of his silent, empty house – suggested that Price could sleep there until he moved.

Price looked across the table at the doctor. He was an old hand at surviving alone, after so many years in the impersonal life of a single man in the Forces. He was so used to looking out for himself, for estimating what there was for Price in every deal, that this offer had to be looked at from all sides.

He tried to size up John Hardy and get under his skin to see what sort of man – and potential employer – he was likely to be. Price saw a compact, self-assured person, yet one who never let his self-assurance grow into arrogance. Perhaps he was a little 'square' – a bit of a 'betsy', as they used to say when Price was young. *Hard to think that he was married to a much younger woman*, thought Price – *this Hardy was cut out to be a bachelor, like me.*

This Hardy was straight, too straight to cut any corners and take short cuts to success. But he seemed a genuine bloke and why not give it a try, just for a bit, anyway?

'Live in *your* house, you mean?'

John Hardy, surprised at himself now, nodded.

'There are five bedrooms in the dashed place. Five! I can only use one at a time, so why not use one of the others. There'll be a lot of work to be done when I move, so it would mean you were on the spot.' He coughed, embarrassed that he might seem to be too eloquent. 'Of course, this is only a stopgap arrangement, until I get settled in the Thames Valley somewhere.'

'OK, Doctor. Fine by me. I'll pay my way, naturally.'

Hardy shrugged. 'Not much to pay for, Mr Price. I almost always eat out, except for the odd snack. Just a place to sleep, I'm afraid, since my wife … died.'

Price saw the wound that the mention of Hardy's wife had opened and adroitly turned the conversation.

'The Group Captain was dead chuffed about that affair in Germany. Got them right off the hook, so I heard. The Sergeant's Mess gets to know everything that DI6 knows – and a lot more besides.'

Hardy nodded, pleased at the memory of the whole episode.

'Any idea what it was all about? Why did the poor fellow vanish from Wales in the first place?'

'Oh, it turns out that he'd gone a bit odd, to say the least. They found out that he had been going to a private doctor for depression – getting some tranquillisers from him. The regular MO at the base didn't know a thing about it. Monks must have just pushed off and gone abroad to kill himself. I've known that happen before.'

Hardy nodded. 'Not uncommon, I agree. Sometimes

people will try to hide themselves away when they decide to end it all. Must have put the wind up the Ministry of Defence, though.'

Price seemed delighted at the thought of the panic in Whitehall.

'I've had a few dealings with that lot myself, in years gone by. They always imagine the worst – and not one of them trusts the other. But it all seems to have come out in the wash, thanks to you and Wingco Loftus. No doubt it was Colin Monks and no doubt he drowned. I suppose the KGB could still have pushed him into the river, but it seems to have satisfied the Intelligence boys.' He took a swig of beer from his glass. 'But I liked that diatom test, I really did. Have you got any more tricks like that up your sleeve?'

'There are a few – not that they always work as well as that one. I wish I had something as effective for this case I'm involved in here.'

John Hardy began to tell him about the Monty Lever affair. Price – who never volunteered his Christian name at any time and seemed content to live without it – listened carefully.

'This Lever chap sounds a right villain. He ought to get the chop for this.'

'He might deserve it – but with such an enthusiastic defence as his solicitor has organised, I'm wondering if they can pull something unexpected out of the hat at next Monday's committal proceedings.'

'What can they say that would be different to your version, Doc?'

Hardy considered this again – he had been over it a number of times in his own mind during the week and was glad to tell it to someone else, helping it to fall into order in his own brain.

'Time of death, probably they'll have a lot to say about that. Monty Lever has an alibi for a certain length of time and I've put the time of death in such a wide bracket that they can't cover it all with his alibi. The other thing might be the cause of death.'

'The asphyxia by that plastic bag?'

'Yes. I'm quite happy about it, but the bag wasn't actually on the girl's head and I'm sure my elder colleague on the defence side will have something to say about it.'

Hardy was careful not to criticise old Glanville West to a non-medical person like Price, though the astute technician immediately guessed that all was not well on the professional front.

'Anything I can do to help in this one, Doc?' he asked. Hardy sipped at a glass of wine and shook his head.

'The Home Office Laboratory have done the blood groups and things like that. I've had the histology processed by my university laboratory and I've been through it all. Not that there's much help there, one way or the other.'

He didn't say that he had an ominous feeling that all was not going to go well in what should have been a straightforward case.

It was obvious from the first that the defence were going to fight tooth and nail to get the case thrown out by the magistrates, to prevent it going for trial.

A leading barrister was briefed for even these preliminary proceedings and though no wigs and gowns were worn in the court, there was an air of excitement and intensity that should have been reserved for the Crown Court.

It was the same room as the one in which the coroner's inquest had been held on Joyce Daniels, but now it was almost full of people. The defence had asked for the lifting of the usual ban on Press reporting, so seven or eight reporters were jammed into the small Press box. Three magistrates sat on the upper dais and the clerk of the court occupied the next lower level. In the dock, Monty Lever sat impassively between two sleepy-looking prison officers. The pews immediately below him carried an unusually dense crowd of lawyers, the one from the Director of Public Prosecutions and his barrister on one side and Saul Bannerman's cohorts on the other.

When Hardy was called to give evidence, he looked around the big room as he walked to the witness box and thought that only the absence of a jury and the wigs of the lawyers made it any different from a trial itself.

Normally, he sat in court while waiting to give his own evidence, but this time the defence had objected, so he was obliged to hang about in the large foyer for several hours. He drank several cups of tea that he didn't really want and grumbled to a policeman about the work he could have done back at the University, if he had been called later.

It was midday before he went into the witness box and had the prosecuting counsel lead him rapidly through his evidence. He told the court of his finding of the body, his estimate of the time of death, the injuries on the body, the asphyxial cause of death and the finding and significance of the plastic bag.

As soon as the barrister sat down, Adam Quayle QC stood up and began a bitter cross-examination. It was most unusual for cross-examination to be started in the magistrates' court, rather than at the trial. But this time, the defence were bursting their blood vessels to ensure that the magistrates would be so unimpressed by the strength of the prosecution's case, that they would dump the case overboard.

'Dr Hardy, with respect to the time of death you have given a very wide range – an extraordinarily wide range, if I might say so.'

Adam Quayle was a large, fat barrister, with jowls and a down-turned mouth that reminded Hardy of the old film actor, Charles Laughton. He had crossed swords with Quayle a number of times in the past and though the man had an overbearing, pompous manner – reminiscent of the old blood-and-thunder counsel of years ago – he had a penetrating mind and cunning turn of speech. A witness had to keep his wits about him to avoid falling into the yawning traps that Adam Quayle was able to build along the path of cross-examination.

Hardy knew that the time of death was to be one of the main lines of attack, because of Monty Lever's carefully contrived alibi.

'My wide time bracket was set in the knowledge of the gross uncertainty of estimating the time of death,' he said carefully.

Quayle rolled his eyes around the court, as if to canvass sympathy for himself in having to deal with such an idiot.

'Dr Hardy,' he said softly. 'I appreciate that we cannot expect the time to be determined to the nearest minute. But surely, in this age of scientific progress, we can hope for something better than you saying – and I quote from your statement – "death probably took place between eight in the evening and four o'clock in the morning"?'

The last words rose in a crescendo, all the more dramatic for the soft beginning.

Hardy was unmoved. 'I think that a very fair estimate. If anything, it errs on the side of too great a restriction. If it were put to me, I could not deny that death took place a couple of hours outside that bracket. That is why I deliberately inserted the word "probably" into my report.'

Chew that one over, Adam, he thought.

Quayle again gave his impression of a man saddened by the mental deficiency of another. For ten minutes, he argued, cajoled and pleaded with Hardy to admit that no experienced forensic pathologist could be so stupid, stubborn or plain ignorant as to believe that the time of death could not be fixed more exactly than to the nearest eight hours. But Hardy was like the Rock of Gibraltar. He was on ground as solid as that rock and quietly, politely yet resolutely, refused to be drawn into any admission that was contrary to his original statement.

Eventually the fat barrister abandoned the subject, but only after a grim threat that 'We shall see, Dr Hardy!'

The rest of the period before the magistrates started looking anxiously at the clock was devoted to probing Hardy's cause of death. Asphyxia was admitted – it could hardly be denied in the circumstances – but then Quayle began to give Hardy a hard time over the matter of the plastic bag.

'You saw the bag on the dead girl's head, Doctor?' he asked innocently.

John Hardy was annoyed, but kept it well concealed.

'It is obvious from my statement and my evidence-in-chief that I did not,' he said sharply. The corners of Quayle's mouth dropped equally sharply.

'Then how do you know it had been over her head and had caused death?' he snapped.

There was blood, mucus and saliva inside it, of the same blood group as the girl's.'

'Did you perform those tests.'

'No, I did not.'

'Are you saying that because the groups were the same, it must be the same person?'

Hardy shook his head. 'No, I've never said that.'

'So they could be totally different persons?'

'Yes. If you wish to indulge in extreme coincidences.'

This nettled Adam Quayle.

'Are "extreme coincidences", as you call them, the province of a medical witness, Doctor?'

'Certainly. When they concern the presence of fresh biological fluids lying within a few feet of a body with the same groupings.'

'*Indeed*, Dr Hardy.' The Queen's Counsel was using heavy sarcasm now. 'Would you tell us what group this blood was?'

Hardy gave a kind of internal sigh. He knew word for word what the next few sentences would be on either side. He had been through it all half a dozen times in other trials.

'It was Group O.'

'Quite. And will you tell the court what is the most common group of all, please?'

'It is Group O.'

'And the Rhesus group, Doctor?'

'It was Rhesus-positive.'

'And the most common Rhesus type is …?'

'Positive.'

'In other words, you couldn't get a more common blood group than this, if you tried for a year?'

'There *were* sub-groups determined, as well.'

'I didn't ask you that, Doctor. Please answer the question.'

'Very well. It was the most common blood group.'

'And now, these sub-groups. Were they common?'

'Well, yes, though each group used reduces the exclusion limits.'

'Were they the most common combination of sub-groups possible?'

'That's not a fair question. I've just said that the more groups that are used, the more specific one can be in excluding a different origin for the blood.'

Quayle smiled sweetly at Hardy.

'And I'm not disputing that, Doctor. I'm asking a different question … even including all the sub-groups you are *so* devoted to, *is* this the most common combination possible?'

Hardy had to admire the way he handled the matter. There was no other answer but, 'Yes.'

The rumbling of the magistrates' stomachs must have reached a crescendo, for the chairman – there was no stipendiary magistrate in Norton Heath – leaned across the bench.

'Will you be much longer, Mr Quayle, or should we adjourn for lunch?'

Quayle looked like a fat cat who had just swallowed a brace of mice.

'I've no further questions, thank you.'

Hardy left the court and went back to his office. He felt uneasy about this whole damned case.

Three days later, his unease changed to incredulity and then outrage.

He was in his laboratory at the house, busy going through some of the techniques on bone with Price. The front doorbell rang.

'I'll get it, you carry on with that,' he said to his new assistant, who was carefully adding caustic soda to a complicated apparatus used for measuring the nitrogen in bone samples.

On the door step he found Alice, looking extremely sour.

'I was just passing through Warwick, on my way back from Norton Heath,' grunted the CID chief. 'Thought I'd call by and tell you the news.'

Hardy took him through to the laboratory before this news was imparted. Carrol nodded briefly at Price, after Hardy had introduced them, then got to the reason for his call.

'Monty Lever has got off!' he said bluntly.

Hardy stared at him. 'Good God, are the magistrates out of their minds?'

Lewis Carrol shook his head ponderously. 'Can't say I altogether blame them. Our evidence looked lousy in court, compared with what the defence threw up. Especially the medical side,' he added pointedly.

Hardy felt his face reddening. 'I must admit, prosecuting counsel didn't make any sort of challenge when Quayle cross-examined me. Our fellow kept saying that they'd thrash all that out at the trial.'

'Well, there ain't going to be no trial, as they say,' snapped Alice. 'It was a cock-up from start to finish. That blasted barrister on our side let the defence get away with anything. As you say, he was saving himself for the trial … the trial we're not going to have now.'

Hardy was bewildered. 'I know it was a fairly circumstantial case. But good God, Mr Carrol, I've seen far worse cases than that sent to the Crown Court.

Carrol fished in his overcoat pocket and pulled out a folded newspaper.

'Here – the local Norton Heath rag. Read what that old codger Glanville West had to say. It'll make your hair curl.'

The morning paper that covered that area had made quite a meal of the court proceedings. The whole of the second page was devoted to the Monty Lever case, with the headline *FAMOUS PATHOLOGIST DESTROYS MURDER EVIDENCE AGAINST NIGHTCLUB OWNER.*

Hardy read with mounting amazement and fury. Price, watching him from a few feet away, expected to see pink froth coming out of his ears by the time he finished reading the report.

'This is outrageous,' spluttered Hardy. 'Diabolical! Why on earth didn't the prosecution ask me to sit in court when this was being given. Surely they cross-examined on all this?'

Lewis Carrol shook his head. 'Hardly a word. And the few words that were said, I'd hate to repeat to you, though they're on that page somewhere.'

He took the paper and poked a large finger at a paragraph towards the end.

'There. Sir Glanville West says that he qualified twenty years before Dr John Hardy and thinks that it is obvious that his much greater experience is self-evident in explaining the difference between their conclusions.'

Hardy was speechless. He had appeared in several hundred homicide cases, but had never seen anything like this.

'The prosecuting counsel should be disbarred, to let them get away with a thing like this. It's preposterous!'

The chief superintendent didn't seem so surprised at the collapse of the case. 'Fair play, Doc, you didn't come across as heavily as old Glanville. He had an answer for everything – the magistrates obviously preferred a firm answer to your hedging your bets.'

Hardy glared at Alice. 'Look, Mr Carrol, you know and I know that exactness is impossible in these things, especially time of death. If I'd have put a firm time on it and it didn't suit the defence, they'd have turned around and said it couldn't be estimated exactly. So how can you win when you've got unscrupulous people on the other side?'

'Use their rules, I should think.'

The new voice was Price, who couldn't resist chipping in.

Carrol grinned, in spite of his bad mood. 'That's it, boy. Play 'em at their own game.'

Hardy looked shocked. 'Certainly not. There's only one truth. I say what I think is right.'

'And you lost,' Carrol reminded him.

'It's not a question of winning or losing. The evidence is as I see it … what the court does with it is their business.'

'So Monty Lever goes free.'

'That's not my responsibility, regrettable though it is. It's the system and unless you want to throw justice out of the window, that's how it's going to stay.'

'Justice! What do you call Lever getting off, to laugh at us? And what about the two dead girls? And maybe the next one he kills, for I'm damn sure he's got a twist in his mind now that'll make him think he can get away with it again.'

Hardy shrugged. 'I know all that, Mr Carrol. But that's not my responsibility. I am engaged to examine the body to the best of my ability – and that's what I did. If you merely want a rigged report, then any constable can do that for you, you don't need a pathologist!'

'I'm not asking you to rig anything, Doc. But how can that other old fellow from India come up with such definite pat answers, that get Lever straight off the hook?'

'Because no one challenged him, that's why,' snapped Hardy, furious with himself now and angry at Carrol for being so obtuse as not to see it. 'That damned lawyer, why didn't he get me to sit behind him and tell him when this Glanville-what's-his-name was talking rubbish?'

Alice started moving towards the door. 'I've got to be off, I only called by to tell you the sad news. I agree that the prosecution are mainly to blame, but they underestimated the defence. That Saul Bannerman's a crafty sod – he's pulled things like this before. That's why half the villains in the Midlands use him. But it's damned hard on people like me sweating my guts out getting a case together, then seeing it melt away.'

Hardy, still fuming, saw the detective to the front door. While he was gone, Price picked up the newspaper and quickly scanned through the press report of the previous day's hearing, when the defence witnesses were in the witness box. There was a whole clutch of people who swore that Monty Lever had not set foot outside the club between ten o'clock on the evening in question and two o'clock the following morning. It was hard to say which of these was lying and which were genuine, but it didn't much matter, as long as their medical witness could put the time of death inside this four-hour bracket. Which he did with apparent relish.

By the time Price got to the doctor's evidence, Hardy had come back into the room. He had cooled off a little, but his rage was now in a steady indignation.

'This Sir Glanville West reckons that she died between eleven o'clock and one in the morning,' said Price, scanning down the columns of the paper.

'Nonsense!' snapped Hardy. 'I didn't take the temperature of the body until about five o'clock the following evening, when she .was virtually down to that of the air.'

Price shrugged. 'This geezer says that the temperature falls at two degrees Fahrenheit each hour, so that gave the time of death at midnight, with an hour each side for a margin of error.'

Rubbish! He can't have read a book on forensic medicine since before the war. Damn it, the girl was lying in a roofless ruined house in a cold October, dressed in a thin blouse and a bit of skirt. There was a wind blowing, the whole place was damp … how on earth can anyone say that the temperature drops at two degrees an hour? I suppose if she'd been in bed under an eiderdown in a centrally heated house, he'd have still used the same ridiculous calculation.'

Price was reading further. 'Now he's saying that his time of death was confirmed by the state of the contents of her stomach. Listen to this – 'she was known to have had a meal of steak pie and chips at nine o'clock that evening. I examined the stomach contents under the microscope and concluded that the state of digestion attained was that which would have been expected after about three hours since the meal.'

Hardy slapped his fist into his palm. 'Absolute rubbish! Rubbish! All that mumbo-jumbo was discredited years ago. Where on earth has this old fossil been, to be so out of touch?'

'India, by what you said, Doc,' replied Price, with a wooden expression. 'There's a bit more here. "When asked his opinion on the cause of death, the well-known professor said that he discounted the allegation that the plastic bag had caused death, as there was no evidence that it had ever been over the girl's head. The so-called blood and mucus could have come from anyone with the most common blood group in Britain and could not be definitely ascribed to the dead girl. Asked for his explanation of the asphyxia, Sir Glanville said that as there had been an appreciable amount of alcohol found in the deceased, she almost certainly suffocated from laying face down on the rubbish on the floor in a drunken stupor and died from obstructing her nose and mouth.".'

'Oh, my God,' groaned Hardy, pacing up and down. 'What utter balderdash! Why on earth didn't our counsel ask me to be there? Or any other sane doctor? "Drunken stupor" indeed! The poor girl only had about a hundred and fifty milligrams of alcohol in her blood.'

Price nodded. '"Almost twice the legal limit for driving a motor vehicle" was how Sir Big-head put it.'

Hardy snorted. 'Indeed! And a fat lot that is, to cause alcoholic coma. I don't know how the magistrates swallowed all this, I really don't.'

'This Sir Glanville West gets a big build-up. That must have impressed them. Forty years' experience, professor in an Indian university. Senior Specialist in the Colonial Service in 1936.'

'Yes, that's about the date he last opened a textbook, I suspect,' snapped Hardy. For him to criticise a medical colleague, even in the privacy of his own home, was a sign of how hard he was pressed.

'Suffocated on the rubbish on the floor! What about that plastic bag, how does he explain that away?'

Price humped his shoulders. 'He doesn't. But he doesn't have to, does he? It's for the prosecution to bring it into the picture.'

Hardy slumped down on to a laboratory stool.

'No good going on about it, I suppose. If this had come

to trial, it would have been a totally different story. With a keen judge there, watching every move and a proper opportunity to cross-examine and lay it all out before the jury, they couldn't pull a string of nonsensical red herrings across the trail like this.'

'What about that other girl you told me about. The one you couldn't find a cause of death for?'

'None of that could be brought into this case, unfortunately. Without any cause of death – not even a stray plastic bag – we hadn't even enough evidence to charge Lever. If the law would allow the prosecution to use the facts of that one to bolster up the evidence in the second death, things would have been very different. But that's the way the law works. It's a safeguard, for all us innocents, I suppose.'

Price grunted. 'It's bloody silly, I think. The coppers know they've got a mad killer sitting in their town and they know who he is. Yet these flaming stupid kid glove rules stop them doing anything about it. If it was me, I'd go up there and shoot him! Save a lot of trouble and expense. Or plant a bit of evidence in his pocket, then arrest him.

Hardy looked profoundly shocked.

'The end never justifies the means, Price. Not if the means are illegal. Britain is what it is because we've always kept on the straight path of the rule of law – and I'd hate to see any change in that.'

'Like the detective said, even if a lot of villains go free?'

'If necessary, yes.'

But the vision of two dead girls trod uncomfortably through his mind as he said it. Were there going to be any more?

Chapter Eight

By the time the Christmas break came along, Hardy's plans for moving had progressed a long way.

His early resolve to cut himself off from Warwick and all its unhappy memories was hardened by a meeting with James Donnington, not long after the outrageous affair of the magistrates' court.

He'd had a short, sharp exchange with Donnington about the reliability of Sir Glanville West, which left neither of the university men in the slightest doubt that any friendship they might have enjoyed was gone forever.

That night, Hardy wrote off to some estate agents in Reading and Maidenhead, asking for details of suitable properties in the Thames Valley.

Next day, he put his own house in the hands of a local property firm and, a month later, his solicitors were beginning the long juggle with draft contracts for the sale of the Warwick house and the purchase of another in Marlow, some thirty miles from central London.

He had given notice to the University of his intention to resign at the end of the three month period and had arranged with Vinton College in Oxford, to take up his part-time appointment there after the Easter vacation.

Now that the die was cast, he was glad of Price to give him both physical and moral support in the awful process of getting ready for the move. Although he still had several months, a glance into the attic of the house told him that there was a fortnight's work above the bedroom ceilings. The garage, too, looked like a museum, and the cupboards of the laboratory concealed things that he would never have dreamed were there.

Over the Christmas period, there was the usual run of impulsive crimes, including a manslaughter after a pub brawl and a killing at a drunken family reunion. But there were no unusual crimes and after a month from the time of the Lever fiasco, John Hardy had begun to hope that he might escape to Marlow before any further trouble came from that direction.

He found Price to be an enigma. He never for a moment regretted his rather impulsive gesture in taking him on, but the man remained a mystery and a challenge to Hardy, whose conventional, tidy mind always liked to classify people that he knew.

Price was both gregarious and a 'loner' at the same time. He enjoyed the company of others; he went to the local public houses almost every night. He played darts, skittles and had the odd flutter on a horse. Yet Hardy noticed that he never drank much – on the couple of occasions when their paths crossed in the evening, he saw that Price always drank half-pints, never a pint, and made them last. He also soon found that Price could be relied upon to keep a tight rein on his mouth. There was never a word about Hardy's professional activities bandied about, though it was a subject that cried out for discussion in any bar parlour. And Price, he also discovered, could look after himself in any spot of trouble. He came home one night with a cut lip and though he passed it off as 'one of the lads got a bit frisky', it got back to John Hardy through his police contacts that Price had sorted out an aggressive and drunken yob who had tried to throw his weight about in the King's Arms that evening.

But Hardy, who was nothing if not a typical product of British public school and university, failed to get to the real depths of Price, to find what made him tick.

He had sensed Price's obstinacy even on the first day he had met him, when his attitude to his senior officers in the Air Force had been one of marginal insolence, just touching the edge of what intuition rather than eyes and ears told him was a bloody-mindedness, perhaps born of a contempt for all authority.

As they got to know each other better, shades of this began to creep into their relationship here in Warwick.

Price was utterly efficient, but there was this hidden undercurrent of stubborn mulishness. If Hardy asked him to do something, Price would often give no sign of even having heard the request and make not the slightest move to get it done. Yet the moment Hardy turned his back, the job would be carried out to perfection, possibly with Price relaxing into a state of indolent laziness by the time that Hardy came to see if it had been done.

It almost became a sort of game between them and Hardy, as tolerant as he was meticulous, accepted the situation.

He never found out a thing about Price's background, family or past life and he was too tactful to enquire. He had discovered his Christian names from the documents necessary for employment but, as Price never responded to anything but 'Price', he gave up using them. He even gave up the 'Mr', as his technician seemed content to be known to the world by a single word.

As the man was a bachelor and a lone wolf, Hardy wondered initially if there might not be something slightly 'queer' about Price – though his appearance was as masculine as one could get.

However, Hardy noticed with satisfaction that Price came home late one night with a smear of lipstick on his collar, a smug expression and a strong smell of a very feminine perfume.

That night, John Hardy lay in his wide, empty bed and wondered about his own sex life. He felt it rather strange that he had no desperate urge to do anything about it.

With the death of Jo, he literally had not even given it a

thought for months. It only came to mind now because of Price's obviously amorous adventures that evening. *Thank God for old age*, thought Hardy. *Perhaps it does release one from the bonds of those excruciating and time-wasting preoccupations that use up half the energy of a young man*. He smiled wryly at the bedroom ceiling as he realised that he was only fifty-five, hardly yet in the realms of impotent senility.

The chain of thought wandered on and he came to a more mundane matter, though one that did have a young woman in it.

When he moved to Marlow, he would need some secretarial help as well as someone intelligent to do some library research for him in connection with his bone research programme.

I must put an advertisement in one of the Reading papers for someone suitable, he thought, as he turned out the light and settled down.

He dreamed that he was being chased up an endless spiral staircase by a body on which he had just performed a post-mortem examination. Try as he would, he was unable to get all the organs back into the abdomen and suddenly the irate corpse had jumped off the stainless steel table and pursued him up the never-ending stairs, which inexplicably turned into a cathedral steeple.

At the top, he dashed in terror into the belfry, where a dozen gigantic bells were clashing out a deafening peal. Then, without any logical change, the bells were ringing the double clangour of a telephone.

Groggily, Hardy realised that his bedside phone was ringing. He stretched out a hand and knocked the whole instrument to the floor.

'Damn the thing … oh my God, who'd be a doctor?' he groaned; as he staggered out of bed and still half asleep groped around the bedroom floor.

He found the receiver and put it to his ear, his eyes

shutting again.

'Dr Hardy? Is that Dr Hardy?'

'It's me. Yes, Dr Hardy.'

'Information Room here, East Mercia Constabulary. Detective Superintendent Partridge asks if you can go urgently to the police station at Norton Heath, sir.

A pang of foreboding went through Hardy and his sleep evaporated instantly. He got very little business from Norton Heath and the name had sinister connotations these past few months.

'Did he say why?'

'They have a body in suspicious circumstances, sir. Officers are at the scene now. I'm calling the Home Office laboratory as well. I don't know any more than that, sir.'

'Right. You can pass a message to the Superintendent that I'll attend as soon as I can get there.'

He rang off and sat on the edge of the bed, rubbing his eyes. Norton Heath. Norton Heath. Is it going to be another? He put his dressing gown on and went along the landing to the room where Price slept. He knocked on the door and immediately an alert voice answered him. Price, he had noticed before, slept like a cat, able to switch on all his faculties instantly.

'We've got a case at Norton Heath. 'D'you want to come? No need if you don't feel like it.'

He wondered if Price's romantic escapades that night had left him exhausted.

'I'll be there right away, Doc. Shall I bring the camera?'

'Yes, if you will. And get my bag from the lab while you're there. I'll be dressed in ten minutes.'

Once again, Hardy was driving the dark roads to a date with violent death. This time he had company in the car, though Price was hardly a talkative companion.

They reached Norton Heath at about three-thirty and went straight into the charge room, where a bevy of large men were standing around, drinking the inevitable police station tea.

Sam Partridge came across the moment they entered the room.

'I don't know if it's the same sort of job, Doctor. It's a girl again, but there's a lot of things different. Mr Carrol is over there now.'

Off they went again, a convoy of cars, but this time travelled no further than the outskirts of the town. Partridge, in the lead police car, picked his way down a road just beyond a council house estate, into a new industrial area which was all chain-link fencing, asbestos-roofed warehouses and tall lamp standards.

The hallmark of police investigation soon came into sight, a cluster of tail and sidelights on a group of vehicles.

This time, the congregation was between two new factory buildings, where a short side road ended blindly in a mound of freshly bulldozed earth.

For once it wasn't actually raining, though it was wet underfoot. The short stub of side road, barely twenty yards long, was barred by a length of white tape from gutter to gutter, in case there were any wheel marks that might be seen in daylight. John Hardy, with Price carrying the bag and camera, followed Sam Partridge along the unmade gravel pavement to the end of the little road. Here it stopped abruptly, with rough scrub dimly visible beyond.

'Morning again, Doctor.'

It was Lewis Carrol, huddled in a padded anorak, standing with half a dozen police officers alongside the waist-high mound of muddy soil.

'Let's have no snags this time, eh?' he added. 'Looks like a straight up-and-downer. In the ditch there.'

Hardy looked down to his right, away from the road. A shallow trench had been excavated by a JCB digger, the earth having been dumped in the line of the roadway. It looked like the bed for sewer pipes or gas mains.

Hardy pulled out the torch he had in his coat pocket and shone it to the ground between the apology for a pavement and the trench. It was a morass of stony mud.

'All right to walk?' he asked automatically.

Carrol turned up his hands. 'Join the club. Half of Norton Heath seemed to have clumped across there tonight – another one won't make much odds.'

With Price close behind, Hardy picked his squelching way to the edge of the trench and looked down.

Two feet below the surface, he saw a completely naked body stretched face up in the soil. Around the feet lapped a few inches of brown water. The arms were behind the back and the eyes stared sightlessly up into his torch beam.

He felt Carrol and Partridge move up behind him. Archie Salmon materialised out of the darkness and grunted a greeting. Even the extrovert scientist seemed subdued – maybe it was the time of day.

'Have we got another the same, then?' grated Alice.

Two other electric lantern beams converged on the body and travelled down to stop between the breasts. There were splashes of reddish mud on the skin, but with the added light, Hardy saw something else.

'She's been stabbed!'

Lewis Carrol bobbed his wrinkled head up and down. 'Four times, as far as we can see without moving her. We've got all our photos.'

Hardy bent down at the edge of the shallow pit. His eyes travelled slowly up and down the length of the corpse for a few moments.

'Take a couple of Polaroids, Price, will you? Just for my own records.'

He stepped back and Price began lighting up the night with his flash gun.

John Hardy turned to the senior officers and the Home Office man.

'I know what you're all thinking,' he said grimly.

'Looks as if she's been knifed, which is a bit out of the usual pattern, if you're trying to bring this one home to Lever again. I can't see any signs of asphyxia on the face.'

'Neither did the first one, remember, Doc. And we couldn't bring in a bloody word about that at the magistrates' court.'

Archie Salmon ran a hand through his steel wool hair.

'What about those arms? They seem in a funny position, tight behind the back like that.'

Hardy nodded. 'I saw that. They might be tied. That'll set us thinking, won't it? As soon as Price has taken a few shots, I'll get down there and turn her over. Do we know who she is yet?'

Sam Partridge answered at once. 'Her clothes were scattered all over the landscape, over there towards the fence.' He waved a hand towards the darkness away from the road. 'Chummy must have run up the top of this pile of muck and slung them as far as he could. Her name was on a tag in her coat; she's a girl from town. Bit of a slag, the lads in the station tell me.'

'Any connection with Monty Lever,' asked Archie.

'Not that we know of – but by damn, if there is, we're going to know it! He's down the station now, sweating it out.'

'Until his blasted smart-alec solicitor gets there,' snapped Alice. 'I'll bet Saul Bannerman hasn't been up at four in the morning for a long time, but he'll be seeing the dawn this day, never fear.'

Price came back to Hardy, placing his feet slowly and carefully, even though all the ground was a hopeless clutter of soggy footprints.

'All done, Doc. What's next?'

Hardy and Archie Salmon went down into the ditch, Price crouching with the police on the edge, holding lights. At close quarters, Hardy checked that there were no signs of asphyxia. Then he looked more closely at the stab wounds, two on the inner side of each breast. There was wet mud around the holes, but little blood.

'Done with a single-edged knife with a broad back,' he said, lifting his head to the detectives above him. 'Maybe something like the old scout's sheath knife.' He poked his torch to within a few inches of the skin. 'One of them has been thrust in right up to the hilt.'

'How do you know?' asked Alice, peering down from the edge of the trench.

'There's a mark at the back end of the wound, from a semi-circular guard at the base of the handle. It can't be a typical scout knife; it must have a projecting piece sticking out about half an inch on the side away from the cutting edge.'

After they had examined all the front of the body, Hardy and the scientific officer turned her over, until she was resting on her side.

'Yes, her wrists are tied together,' reported Archie, who had the best view. 'All muddied up, but it looks like a piece of electric flex.'

'May as well lift her up now, rather than let her fall back into the mud.'

A few moments later, the combined efforts of four men had placed the pallid corpse safely into a cocoon of polythene and, within forty minutes, they were in the familiar surroundings of the hospital mortuary.

This time Hardy got straight on with temperature estimations, his long chemical thermometer registering thirty-one degrees centigrade. He did some rapid mental arithmetic and then balanced the result against the awkward circumstances of the slim girl being found stark naked in muddy water on a January night.

'I'd guess four to seven hours ... that puts it between ten o'clock last night and one this morning,' he decided. 'Though, if you twisted my arm, I'd put another hour either side of that.'

Price took some more photographs, so did the police photographer.

Archie did his routine with Sellotape, then Hardy went to work. Again, there was no mortuary assistant but, without being asked, Price silently donned gown, boots and apron.

'Done it plenty of times, Doc, from Scotland to Hong Kong,' he muttered.

Even through the worry and tension of the problem in hand, John Hardy felt a strengthening of regard for his odd ex-airman. He was a strange chap, but he was what they called a. 'treasure'.

Detective Chief Superintendent Carrol had sent Partridge to attend the post-mortem, while he himself was driven back to the police station at Norton Heath.

In a small interview room, Monty Lever sat impassively smoking a cheroot, waiting patiently for his solicitor to arrive.

Lewis Carrol pushed the door open and walked in, kicking a chair into place on the other side of the small table.

'You're right in it this time, Monty,' he snapped. 'What have you got to say for yourself?'

Lever's round face stared at him insolently, the fringe of beard like a balaclava helmet around his face.

'You'll regret this, when Bannerman gets here. Dragging respectable people from their beds on some trumped-up excuse. Harassment, that's what it is.'

'Shut up. Where were you between ten o'clock last evening and one o'clock this morning?'

'I've got nothing to say, so don't waste your breath and my time.'

'Know a girl called Molly Freeman?'

'Never heard of her. Is she a .friend of yours?'

'Don't act clever, Lever. You're in a spot.'

'I hadn't noticed.'

There was a banging of a door from outside, a pattering of feet and the door was thrown open to reveal Saul Bannerman, looking slightly untidy and unshaven, a most unusual condition for the suave lawyer.

'What's all this about?' he asked.

'I'm busy asking your client here a few questions,' said. Carrol, not getting up.

'And I'm busy not answering them,' said Lever, with a sneer.

Bannerman looked from one to the other suspiciously. 'I'd like a few minutes alone with my client.'

Carrol stared at the opposite wall. 'Hard lines,' he said.

Bannerman reddened. 'I demand to have a consultation with Mr Lever.'

'Go ahead, nothing stopping you, Mr Bannerman.'

'Alone, I mean.'

'Sorry, no dice. I don't want any stories cooked-up behind the scenes.

Bannerman gobbled with indignation. 'That's a most improper remark, Chief Superintendent.'

'Protest noted. Now, I intend carrying on with my questioning of your Mr Lever. You're entitled to be present, that's all.'

But the session was a wash-out, as Alice had expected it to be. Monty Lever either refused to answer or his lawyer jumped in first, to prohibit his reply.

After half an hour of fruitless questioning, Saul Bannerman started his campaign to get Lever out of the station, challenging Carrol to bring a charge or to let Lever go home.

'We're waiting for several bits of additional information. Until they are to hand, he stays. And perhaps for a long time after that,' he added ominously.

He left the room, but detailed a sergeant to stay in the room and record any conversation.

In the CID office, he put a call through to the hospital and spoke to Partridge in the mortuary.

'Any progress, Sam? How's John Hardy coming along?'

Partridge, using the phone in the ante-room outside the actual autopsy room, looked through the open door to where the crowd of people were standing around the open cadaver on the porcelain table.

'He's looking a bit worried at the moment. Hasn't said why, but I've got the feeling he's not very happy about something: She's been raped, properly this time.'

Alice, at the other end of the phone, raised his grey eyebrows up and wrinkled his brow. 'Raped? But she's known for giving it away pretty free ... or at least, for a couple of quid, isn't she?'

Partridge scratched his armpit with his free hand.

'So Williams says; he knows the local tarts. But even a "pro" can be ravished, if she doesn't fancy the guy. And who the hell would fancy Monty Lever?'

'What about this wrist business?'

'Tied deeply, cutting into the skin. Three-core electric flex, the sort you have on a fire or an electric iron. Looks as common as it comes – have a hell of a job tracing it.'

Lewis Carrol grunted into the phone.

'OK. Let me know the minute you've got anything. Williams is hunting round town looking for whoever last saw the girl, though five in the morning is a hell of a time to start a house-to-house. See you.'

Partridge rang off and went back into the inner room.

The body was gutted, an empty shell with all the organs now dissected on a flat table alongside the sink. Hardy was thoughtfully running water over the heart and lungs from a length of rubber pipe attached to the cold water tap.

'Can you stand a surprise, Mr Partridge?' he asked.

Sam felt a hand grab at his stomach. *Oh God, don't foul it up again, Dr Hardy*, he silently prayed.

Aloud, he said suspiciously, 'Depends what the surprise is.'

John dropped the pipe and turned round.

'She wasn't stabbed,' he announced bluntly.

Sam stared at him. 'She bloody was! Sorry, Doc, but she was. I mean, we can all see them!'

Hardy lifted a hand. 'I should have said, she wasn't stabbed *to death*. She was already dead when she was knifed.'

There was silence in the room, as six men stared at him.

'Then what the blazes did she die of?' asked Partridge, already visualising himself passing the news on to Alice.

'I don't know. I just don't know.'

'Oh Christ, Doc. Not again!'

Hardy shrugged. 'Sorry, but I can't manufacture what isn't there. But putting the two previous cases together, we can surely build up a pattern which implicates a plastic bag. We've got the tied wrists, the "no cause of death" in the first, the asphyxia in the second, and now tied wrists and "no cause" in this one.'

'But what about the stabbing?'

'I think it's a red herring. Done after death, just to confuse the issue and alter the modus operandi.'

Sam took a minute to digest this. 'Alice will blow a gasket when he hears this,' he muttered.

He looked up, grasping at straws.

'How can you tell that she was stabbed *after* death?'

'All the knife wounds have penetrated into the chest, but there's not a ha'p'orth of bleeding. One of them has opened the aorta, the great main blood vessel, but there's hardly a spoonful of blood in the chest cavity. If she'd been alive, there'd have been a torrent of blood.'

'How long after death was she stabbed?'

'Impossible to tell. Could be a minute, could be an hour.'

Archie Salmon, who had been busy fiddling with swabs from the vagina, little packets with tufts of pubic hair and all the other accoutrements of his trade, looked up cheerily.

'Full-blown rape, this time. You can tell Alice that; it'll help to soften the blow.'

Sam rolled his eyes to heaven and walked out to the telephone.

Chapter Nine

Price sat at the bar of the Saracen, a lager in front of him bought at almost twice the price it would have been in the King's Arms. He had a gaudy tie around the neck of a shirt patterned in small flowers and his suit, bought in Singapore some years ago, was just a shade too blue for good taste.

This was the second night running that he had forsaken his local pubs for the doubtful delights of the Norton Heath nightclub. A few weeks earlier, he had bought a somewhat beaten-up Ford Escort and this had brought him from Warwick to do some snooping at Monty Lever's fun palace.

The sole attractions seemed to be the red decor, the ear-splitting music and the easily available female talent that was scattered about the two rooms downstairs.

He wondered about what went on upstairs, though so far he had seen no sign of any of the girls sidling in that direction. A few men had vanished up to the first floor and he suspected that there might be an unlicensed casino somewhere, but that was of no interest to him.

It was the female talent that attracted him, mainly in the line of duty.

One of them was sitting next to him now, a rather cheeky brunette who had conned him into buying her a rum and pep as the first shot in some bargaining.

They had got past the small talk and exchange of names. Price knew that the girl would be anxious to get down to some more definite proposition soon. It was almost midnight, but if they struck a bargain now, she might get back again in time for another customer before the place closed in the early hours.

But Price was not as eager. He had come for information and he began to spin out the talk in that direction.

'Expect you meet some funny guys in here?' he began.

She looked suspiciously at him. 'What d'you mean – funny?'

'Well, wanting something a bit different. You know!'

He gave her a leer and a wink at the same time.

The brunette looked coldly at him. 'Don't know what you mean.'

The barman came over and looked pointedly at Price's glass, which he had just drained. The girl quickly threw down her own drink and banged the glass down on the bar.

Price took the hint. 'Same again.'

He'd had a few words with the barman the previous night, when the thick-set bruiser who dispensed the drinks had glowered at him at the end of the night and asked him bluntly if he was 'a bleeding copper'. During the few weeks since the last murder, the police had been in and out of the Saracen like yo-yos, according to the barman. It took a couple of drinks and some fast talking from Price to satisfy the man that he was not 'the fuzz'. The man's suspicions seemed to have returned tonight and Price realised that he would have to step carefully. He grinned to himself as he thought of John Hardy's face if he knew his laboratory technician was snooping around on his behalf.

The old man would have a stroke, thought Price. *He's so straight that the thought of a bit of underhand work would outrage him beyond measure.*

Price brought himself back to the business in hand and again started chatting up the girl. They ground their way through a halting dialogue, until the girl began looking at her watch and throwing hopeful looks around the room. But there were few people there and no other unattached males. She decided that half a man in the hand was worth two in the bush and turned back to Price again.

'Monty Lever owns this place, doesn't he?' asked Price, trying to steer the conversation the way he wanted.

'So they say. What time have you got to go?' answered the girl.

'Oh, I'm in no hurry. I like it here.'

'I've got a little flat not far away. Know what I mean?'

Price did, but he couldn't spend half of every night in a girl's bed. It was costing too much for one thing. He had ended up in one last night, with an enthusiastic amateur, and though he hadn't been too distressed by the experience, it hadn't got him any further on the road to finding out about Lever's habits and movements.

'I've got a car. Just down the road.' He threw this in as a possible detonator. It got some results.

'No thank you. There's been too much trouble in cars round here lately. It's my place or nothing,' she snapped.

'What d'you mean, trouble in cars? With who?'

'Forget it. And forget your car, too, see.'

Price tried to play dumb. 'I don't get it, gorgeous. You don't mean you're scared of guys in cars? Is it all this fright about killings that worries you?'

'I said, forget it.'

She seemed to be staring past him over the bar and he turned his head to see the barman standing with Durrant, the manager, at the opposite end. They were looking down towards them and they didn't look happy. Suddenly, the girl picked up her handbag and jumped off the bar stool.

'I've got to go. See you.'

She walked quickly away, before Price could say anything to her. He watched her bottom wiggle across the room in her tight skirt, until she vanished out of sight around the corner of the peninsula-shaped bar.

Price shrugged and picked up his drink. He could still see the two men watching him from the corner of his eye.

It looked as if the evening was going to be a dead loss again. There was another girl sitting alone over against the wall, but he decided to wait a bit before making any more obvious move.

The same had happened three nights ago, when he went to a club of Lever's in Solihull, nearer Birmingham. After a few attempts at chatting up the staff and the resident girls, everyone seemed to have a sharp attack of tight mouths.

He looked at his watch again. *Twenty past midnight.* He hunched over his Tuborg and decided to call it a night after he had finished this one. His clever idea to help the old man was turning out as useful as a lead balloon.

Price went over the sequel to the surprising post-mortem, now almost three weeks before. The girl had been badly raped, bruised and torn, even though she was no stranger to sex, to put it mildly. The stab wounds had been confirmed as post-mortem and the cause of death could only be inferred from the two previous cases, if one subscribed to the view that a plastic bag might have caused asphyxia. This was not a universal view, as the discharge of Monty Lever by the magistrates had confirmed.

Once again, Saul Bannerman had exhumed the old professor to do a second post-mortem. This time, John Hardy had kept well out of the way, not risking a snub by offering to clarify his findings at the first autopsy.

Neither Hardy nor anyone else knew what conclusions the ex-colonial pathologist had dreamed up. This was the privilege of the defence, who could keep all their evidence – except that of alibi – up their sleeve right until the moment they went into the witness box, whereas the prosecution had to make everything available to the defence in advance.

So far, no one had been charged with the murder of Molly Freeman, and the Press, both local and national, were kicking up quite a dust. Bold headlines like *TREBLE*

SLAYING GOES UNSOLVED! and *NO CAUSE OF DEATH, SAYS DOCTOR* were appearing in the newspapers, with acid editorials wondering what the police and forensic services were coming to.

Hardy had retired into a silent shell, but Price could tell that he was taking the publicity badly. Not that newspaper stories had any impression on him, but it was the hurt looks of his police friends and the implied reflection on the forensic art that stung his professional pride.

An inquest had been opened, and again Hardy had to say that the cause of death was not apparent. Due to the fact that a police investigation was going on and might well come to a criminal trial, he could not go into the circumstantial matter of the similarity between the previous murders. This was no part of the coroner's function, especially at an opening of the inquest, without a jury.

So, poor John Hardy was stuck firmly between two stools, unable to give a firm decision, yet unable to vindicate his position by a full explanation of the circumstances.

He took refuge in an aloof silence, going soft-footedly about his business and preparing to move away from Warwick and all its unfortunate associations of the past few months.

This wasn't good enough for Price, however. In his taciturn way, he had become very fond of Hardy. He felt that he owed him a debt for the ready berth he had given him on leaving the Air Force. To Price, debts were meant to be repaid promptly and he set about it with typical directness.

Problem – the police had insufficient evidence to charge Lever, who was the obvious villain of the piece. Answer – find them some evidence! As they had got nowhere by legal means, then use illegal ones. Price's occasional adventures in the Forces had given him both the psychological attitude and some of the technical knowledge to do this sort of thing and he was quite ready to give it a try.

Through things that Hardy had learned from the detectives and also from some pub talk with a local police sergeant that Price had known years ago in the RAF, he knew that the investigation had failed to find any link between the last victim, Molly Freeman, and the bearded owner of the Saracen Club. Once again, Lever had an alibi provided by his henchmen for all the period during which the girl could have died and there was no physical evidence to connect him, or his cars with the scene of the crime. The same blood group had been found in the semen in the girl as in the previous killings, which matched that of Monty Lever, but this was quite insufficient evidence on its own.

What was needed was some firm connection between Lever and the girl, which explained Price's midnight excursions around Lever's clubs.

So far, he had gained nothing at all. As soon as he began exploring the subject with any of the hostesses or bar girls, they clammed up. Price guessed, correctly, that they had either been warned off or were just too scared to open their mouths.

The only slight clue he had gained was from the girl he took home the previous night, who had let slip that she had once been out with Lever –who, although he threw his money around freely, 'was just too damn kinky for her'. She seemed to sense that she had already said too much and nothing would persuade her to say any more.

That was the stage he had reached on this particular night when he decided to give up and go home, as soon as he reached the bottom of his beer glass.

He'd had a few more to drink than he had planned. Normally, two pints a night was his limit. He could take more, far more, but he had learned in the Sergeant's Mess that drunks were just damn fools. It went against his pride to lose control of himself, apart from the fact that he had to drive back home from Norton Heath now and he knew that he was well over the breathalyser limit.

Walk it off for a bit, he decided as he got off the stool and trod with over-deliberate steps to the door. He certainly wasn't drunk, but he had that tell-tale numbness of the forehead, that itself told of a drop too much alcohol circulating through his system.

The cold air outside refreshed him immediately and he walked briskly along the pavement away from the direction in which he had left his car.

'Go round the block to it. Blow the cobwebs off,' he muttered to himself.

There was a light fog and the air was cold and damp, so he thrust his hands deeply into the pockets of his short leather coat.

Putting his hands into his pockets turned out to have been a mistake. He walked two hundred yards along the main street, past darkened shops and dimly lit stores. Then he turned down a narrow side street to reach the road that ran parallel to High Road, his intention being to double back to his car.

There must have been a lane between the two main roads, which led to the back door of the Saracen, for, as he crossed the dark opening, he suddenly heard a scuffing of feet. He whipped round, but before he could pull his hands free, his arms were pinioned and a hail of blows began falling on his face, chest and stomach.

There were no voices, which made it all the more frightening. Price had been in many a brawl in his younger service days, but respectable years as a technician sergeant had put him a little out of practice. The first clouts effectively blocked his vision, as blood began running into his eyes. Gasping from a punch in the stomach, he sagged and the hands that held him suddenly relaxed, letting him fall into a heap on the ground. Before he even hit the pavement, kicks began landing on his arms and body. Thankfully, the feet that delivered them were wearing relatively soft shoes. The same blows with heavy boots might well have killed him.

He was almost senseless by now, partly from pain and partly from fearful surprise, but he still retained enough consciousness to hear the only words that were uttered throughout the whole vicious assault.

'Keep away from the clubs, you bastard, or we'll kill you.'

Then all was silent. The blows went away, but the pain stayed with him. The whole episode couldn't have lasted more than thirty seconds, though it seemed like thirty minutes.

Gasping, Price pushed himself to his hands and knees and promptly vomited from the pain in his stomach. He slumped to a sitting position and crouched for a few minutes huddled over his aching belly. Then he feebly groped in a pocket for his handkerchief and began wiping enough blood from his face to enable him to see.

He sat there for a while, alone in the dark side street. Afraid that a police patrolman might find him and take him for a drunk, he hauled himself shakily to his feet and staggered off back to the main road.

Some way down the street, he found a shop doorway where light from a street lamp turned the glass into a mirror. He looked at himself and groaned. He would have to stop somewhere and try to clean up a bit, in case the old man saw him when he got back to the house – though Hardy should be in bed by now. Thank God they hadn't hit him in the mouth too much. Price was very proud of his teeth.

He plodded on towards his car, feeling weaker at the knees with every step.

As he passed the closed door of the Saracen, he used a

few choice Sergeants' Mess oaths to vow that he would get even with them.

Two days later, John Hardy attended a meeting in the County Police Headquarters.

In Lewis Carrol's office, a top level conference was being held, at which the Assistant Chief Constable (Crime) was present, as well as Alice, Partridge, the Director of the Home Office Forensic Science Laboratory, Hardy, Archie Salmon and the chief guest, a solicitor from the Director of Public Prosecutions in London.

It was rare for the DPP to be involved in a conference before any arrest had been made, but the unusual circumstances had made it necessary. There were now three unsolved murders, a discharged suspect and, not least, the beginnings of a public outcry, being carefully nurtured by the Press. The echoes of the newspapers' protests, had percolated into the normally immune chambers of the Director of Public Prosecutions in Queen Anne's Gate, and a decision on possible action was needed.

'I'll admit, this is the hottest potato we have on the books at the moment,' said Mr Lawson, the lawyer from London. 'The Director wants to weigh up how much evidence we have and how it could possibly be dovetailed together to make a .case out of the whole three killings, if necessary.'

Lewis Carrol wagged his head slowly from side to side. 'Not good at the moment, Mr Lawson. Not good at all. We've got next to damn all on the last one, Molly Freeman. Only the Group B semen, same as the other two.'

Archie Salmon said, 'No blood in any of the vehicles belonging to Lever. No hairs, no nothing. And every time, it's been raining or too messed up for us to get any tyre tracks. Just damn all.'

Lawson, a horn-rimmed civil servant with pale hair brylcreemed into a flat plate on top of his head, turned to Hardy.

'Doctor, you seem to have had a hard time on all these cases. You've got my sympathy. There's little credit to be won by admitting that you don't know.'

Hardy gave him a wry smile. 'Thanks for that, at least. It's been an interrupted nightmare, pathologically speaking. Two "no causes of death" and a stabbing that was nothing to do with death. Awful!'

Lawson nodded. 'But can you fit the three together into a pattern?'

'You mean fill the deficiencies of one case with the information from another?'

'More or less.'

'Certainly, the plastic bag in the Penny Vincent death would explain the other two. Though the legal aspects of transferring a fact into a theory are your province, I'm afraid. But medically, I'd go into the witness box quite confidently to say that death without asphyxial signs could have occurred in Joyce and Molly from a plastic bag being put over the face.'

The Home Office laboratory chief cut in here.

'There's the common denominator of the tied wrists in all cases. Surely that's very valuable in showing that all three deaths were the work of one man? And that because he used a plastic bag in one case, he might equally well have used it in another.'

'Certainly ... we've gripped on to the fact with enthusiasm up at the Office,' said Lawson. 'But the whole edifice is a bit like a pack of cards ... although it holds together, it only needs a breath of wind to knock it all down.'

He waved his hands about like some master architect. 'We need some fresh facts to brace the whole structure together.'

There was a pregnant silence.

'We've *got* no more bloody facts,' said Alice bluntly. Lawson looked pointedly at John Hardy.

'Is there nothing at all that you can produce, Doctor? Anything about the time of death that would let us out of these obviously faked alibis?'

Hardy shook his head. 'Afraid not. I could squeeze an hour or two longer on Penny or Molly, perhaps, but I don't think that would help. No doubt the defence would just happen to remember someone else who would vouch for Lever during that time.'

'You're damn right,' growled Sam Partridge. 'They'd stretch their alibis to fit'

'Nothing on the forensic science side?' asked Lawson.

Archie shrugged helplessly. 'Not so much as a whisker. We combed out the pubic hair of all the victims to try to find a different foreign strand that might match Lever, but nothing. No skin under the nails of any of the girls, which might have indicated that one of them might have scratched his face.'

'The hands tied behind their backs would account for that,' said Alice.

There was another silence.

'And nothing we can do with the knife?' asked Lawson.

The knife had been found two days later by a thorough police search of the rough scrub behind the place where the last girl, Molly Freeman, had been found. It had obviously been thrown from the edge of the side road and its heavy handle had carried it a long way.

'It was exactly like Dr Hardy prophesied,' granted Lewis Carrol. 'A one-edged bowie knife with a projecting guard on the handle. Had the girl's blood on it, but no fingerprints. Nothing at all to connect it with Lever. We've had photographs of it toted all over the Midlands for a week, but no one recognises it in any context of our suspect.'

'And you think, Doctor, that the stabbing was done after death?'

'I don't *think*, Mr Lawson, I'm certain. I feel that it was done as an attempt to confuse us when the body was found – to make it look as if it was a crime unrelated to the previous ones.'

'Some hope, if all the girls had their wrists tied,' muttered Alice.

The lawyer seemed to look to Hardy for most of his information.

'This tying of the wrists. How do you interpret that, Doctor. You've seen it before, no doubt?'

Hardy pondered a moment. 'I think it might have two reasons. Firstly, as a means of immobilising the girl, to make forcible intercourse easier. Secondly, as a definite act of perversion. I don't need to tell you that bondage, tying, manacles and ropes are a very significant part of sadomasochistic sexual activities.'

'Commonly known as "kinky", Doc,' said Carrol. 'I think that was the main thing here. Let's face it, none of these girls was any innocent virgin. They were either enthusiastic amateurs or part-time whores. The last one certainly was; she had a conviction for soliciting, two years ago in Birmingham.'

'You think they wouldn't have been unwilling?' suggested Lawson.

'Well, willing enough for a bit of fun in the back seat – though how any of them could stomach Monty Lever, I don t know. That's about the only point in his favour, the doubt that any girl would go with him.'

'He used to flash his money about, that's the answer,' said Sam. 'We've got a couple of girls who used to hang about his clubs who'll say that they've been with him in the past and he was a good spender.'

'You reckon they didn't bargain for any kinky stuff and

when they protested, he whacked a bag over their head, then tied 'em up?' Archie voiced the general way that their thoughts were going.

John Hardy nodded. 'Sounds reasonable enough. But it doesn't help us get any nearer those extra facts that are needed to bring him to trial.'

'One bit more evidence,' growled Alice. 'One good fact, that's all we need!'

Price was determined to get that fact, if he had to brain every one of Lever's strong-arm men to get it.

Five days after he had suffered the attack in the back street, he made preparations to do some burglary. He used part of the time that John Hardy paid him to work in the laboratory, in collecting a set of housebreaking tools. He emptied the surgical instruments out of a canvas roll that the doctor used to use before he had his smarter black bag, then filled the pockets with an assortment of gadgets.

Long-nosed pliers, bits of strong wire, a sheet of celluloid, an old Barclaycard, a small hand drill and a few strong screwdrivers and chisels were carefully wrapped in the canvas so that they did not rattle.

He hid this in the boot of his battered Escort and waited for the late evening.

Price's face still showed a few scratches and he had a black eye on one side, though the swelling had now gone down.

He had got into the house unnoticed that night and had patched himself up, to the best of his ability. In the morning, he had explained his battered face to Hardy by spinning some tale of a brawl in a public house, in which he had gone to the assistance of the landlord against a crowd of drunken yobs. Hardy seemed to have taken the story without too much suspicion and the whole thing had been forgotten. Price could sense that Hardy's mind was not too concerned with the state of his laboratory assistant's face. He knew that the continuous niggling in the Press about the murders was preoccupying the pathologist.

From the telephone book, Price had found that Lever lived in a flat at Knowle, a small town between Norton Heath and Birmingham.

He drove there at about ten o'clock, when he felt that Lever was most likely to be out at one of his clubs.

Parking the car well away from the address, Price pushed his roll of tools into the deep pocket of an old raincoat and walked back to 'case' the place.

It was ideally situated for break-in, being in one of half a dozen luxury blocks set in a large garden-like area just off the main road. There were plenty of trees to shade the doorways from street lamps. Each block of flats contained no more than six or eight residences, being only three storeys high. The approach road that coursed through the gardens passed the end of Lever's block, alongside some detached garages that served the flats.

Price feared that there might be a common outer door that might be locked but, as he walked up to the building, he saw that each flat had an individual front door. In fact, they were really maisonettes, rather than flats.'

He could see from the structure of the place that number twenty was on the first floor. There were no lights on, unless the curtains were very thick and free from chinks.

To be on the safe side, Price pressed the bell and waited. He heard a distant ringing, but no one came after a full minute. He used the time to study the lock and to press experimentally against the door. It was an ordinary cylinder lock and the door could be pushed inwards slightly to show a gap of a few millimetres between the edge and the door frame.

He deftly slid out part of the Barclaycard, which he had cut longways with shears, getting rid of the raised, embossed figures that would interfere with his operation.

He had a quick look over his shoulder to make sure that it was all clear, then heaved forcibly with his shoulder against the door. At the same time he slid the plastic strip into the crack at the level of the lock. He had practised this many times before and, within seconds, he had pushed back the tongue of the lock and stepped inside the hallway.

He closed the door quickly and walked quietly up the thickly carpeted stairs.

At the top was an unlocked glass door, leading into another hallway with a number of closed doors leading off.

He had a torch and it showed a decor of such luxury that it amounted to opulence. Lever must have been fond of red and purple. It was like the interior of the Saracen Club.

'Like a ruddy Turkish knocking shop!' he murmured, as he tried the first door. In a few minutes, he had made a quick tour of the deserted flat. The kitchen, bathroom and lounge he left until last, concentrating on the three bedrooms and the study, which was more of an office than anything else.

Two of the bedrooms were lavishly furnished, but had an unused look about them, with very little in the drawers and cupboards. The third and largest was undoubtedly Monty's own room. Huge built-in wardrobes were filled with expensive clothes, one part containing women's nightdresses and underclothes.

The room was very sex orientated, with a gigantic treble-sized four-poster bed, having a large mirror fixed to the underside of the canopy. There were several large gilt mirrors standing around the room and on the velvet-papered walls were several large and erotic pictures.

With one ear listening for any interruptions, Price went to work on the drawers and cupboards. He knew that the police had searched this flat at the time of Monty's abortive arrest following the second killing, but that was some time ago. He hoped that something might have been imported since then, that could help to incriminate him.

Many of the drawers held nothing but clothes, expensive shirts and underwear, but at the bottom of a bedside cabinet, he found a pile of magazines. Some were mere 'girlie' books, but lower in the pile were hard porn books, most of them continental in origin. Price leafed through them rapidly, and noticed that the predominant theme was bondage and masked performers.

'Dirty sod!' he muttered and took one of the hottest publications as a sample, rolling it up and stuffing it into the pocket of his coat.

He had been in the flat for twenty minutes now. There seemed nothing else in the main bedroom and, very rapidly, he whipped through all the other rooms except the bathroom and kitchen, looking into cupboards and passing his eye rapidly over the books on the bookcases. There was a safe m the office, but it was well beyond his ability to crack. He hoped it only contained money. There was a filing cabinet, but that seemed to be legitimate place for nothing but the business side of Lever's activities. Maybe a tax inspector might find it interesting, but it seemed to have nothing in it for Price.

It took the better part of an hour to skin the flat and at the end of it, all he had to show for his toil was one dirty book. But something about that bedside cabinet seemed to call to him.

He went back to it and again pulled out all the magazines, going through each one to make sure that nothing was hidden inside the pages. He got to the last one without so much as a bus ticket falling out. Disappointed, he crouched on the floor, wondering if there was anything more he could do.

As he stared into the empty cupboard, alongside the silk fringe of the bedcover, his unfocused eyes slowly began to see something. Inside the cupboard, the floor was covered with Formica, but he noticed that the laminate did not quite reach the edges. There was a big central square, with an inch border all round.

Price put a hand down and gripped the edge of the crack with his fingernails. The floor of the cabinet came up easily and showed him a space three inches deep, resting on the planks of the bedroom floor itself. In the cavity was a jumble of books, papers and photographs.

His heart jumped, as he realised that here was a hoard that might contain gold.

He grabbed the untidy heap of paper and dumped it onto the carpet, rapidly flipping through it to see what was there.

There were a few picture books of a degree of obscenity that made even Price's hardened eyes open a bit wider. Many of them were of a sadomasochistic nature. A handful of 'commercial' photographs were of the same ilk. But much more interesting were a number of Polaroid photographs, both colour and black and white. Price had noticed a camera of this type in a cupboard in the office.

They were almost all of a poor technical quality – *obviously taken by an amateur – and*, he thought, *a highly excited amateur with a shaky hand*! But what they lacked in clarity, they made up for in content. Several girls were involved and, in almost all of them, the scene was the same bedroom that Price was in at the moment. A couple of others were in the open air and two were taken inside a motor car.

All showed the girls in various stages of undress, down to complete nakedness and all displayed a variety of sadomasochistic poses, most of them with bondage by ropes and cords.

In three of the pictures – apparently taken with a time-lapse device on the camera – a man was involved. Two of them showed nothing recognisable except a large expanse of bare male skin, but the third had the unmistakable figure of Monty Lever as one of the two participants.

What riveted Price's attention, however, was not the crude eroticism of the photographs, but the fact that the girl in two of them was Molly Freeman!

She was not actually with Lever in the same picture, but Price's face split into a triumphant grin as he realised the significance of the find. He looked carefully through the other photographs to try to recognise either of the other dead girls. He had seen copies of police photographs that Hardy had at the laboratory, but could not identify either of them in the Polaroids.

With one ear cocked for sounds outside, he squatted alongside the cupboard and thought rapidly about the potential use of this discovery in nailing Monty Lever.

Lever had categorically denied ever having known Molly Freeman, so these photographs, if traced to his hidden cache, would give the lie to that. They would also establish his predilection for grotesque forms of sex, consistent with the tying of the dead girls.

'These should sink the swine!' muttered Price, but then he started to wonder how the pictures could legitimately be got into the hands of the police. He had been more than willing to do a bit of snooping and a touch of breaking-and-entering in the cause of getting Hardy's reputation back on the rails, but he was not enough of a martyr to let himself be caught as a thief in the night.

He pondered for a moment, then his nimble mind thought of the perfect answer.

Chapter Ten

Hardy sat through the whole trial, from beginning to end. It was only a matter of days before he was due to move house to the Home Counties. He had given up all his work at the University and there was little point in carrying on with more police and coroner's work in the Warwick area, as he would be living a hundred miles away by the time fresh cases came to court.

The Lever trial was relatively soon after the club owner's arrest, in fact a little more than two months. It was held in Worcester Crown Court, at the old Assize Hall in the main street, with the great antechamber which was more spacious and impressive than the old courtroom itself.

He sat now in the second row of benches near the front of the court, alongside Lawson, the solicitor from the Director of Public Prosecutions.

Immediately in front of him were the two prosecution barristers, led by Barnes Campbell QC. At the other end of the same row, Saul Bannerman and the angular form of Sir Glanville West sat in similar positions behind counsel for the defence – again dominated by Adam Quayle.

Price sat in the public gallery, determined not to miss a word of the proceedings. He was secretly revelling in the fact that, apart from one other person, not a soul knew that he alone was responsible for all this complex and expensive performance that was taking place below him.

The Press box was jammed tight and the public seats around Price were filled to capacity. Alongside the learned judge, the other chairs on the high rostrum were taken by local dignitaries who were using their positions of authority to make sure of a ringside seat.

There had been a long conference in the law chambers of Barnes Campbell a few days before and another session before the trial began that morning.

It was now early afternoon, most of the morning having been taken up by all the necessary preliminaries of swearing-in a jury and a long opening speech by the prosecuting counsel, outlining the facts of the case.

Then there had been the rather dreary routine evidence given by the police photographer to prove all the albums of pictures, the same proof of various maps and plans drawn by a police draughtsman and a straightforward identification by the tearful mother of the last victim, Molly Freeman.

Monty Lever was charged with the murder of all three girls, though the bulk of the evidence was concentrated on the last one, Molly Freeman. The Director of Public Prosecutions had decided on this course of action so that the similarities of the three cases could be brought to the notice of the jury, in order to strengthen the case against Lever in respect of Molly. If the first two cases had not been included in the indictment, the defence would inevitably have fought – and fought successfully – to have the evidence of the earlier cases kept out of evidence.

Monty Lever had been dismayed, when he had an urgent consultation with Saul Bannerman, to find that he was going to be charged with the killing of the second girl, Penny Vincent.

'What the hell sort of lawyer are you?' he snarled. 'I thought that once somebody was acquitted on a charge, he couldn't be done again for the same offence?'

Saul Bannerman shook his head sadly.

'Sorry, Monty. Doesn't apply here.'

The bearded club owner became livid.

'Is there a different law for me than for the rest of the

bloody population, eh? I was discharged by the magistrates, wasn't I?'

Bannerman kept on shaking his head. 'The magistrates weren't trying you, Monty,' he said patiently. 'To be free of a charge, whether you did it or not, you have to be tried. And in murder, that means at Crown Court. The justices had no power to do that, they were only deciding whether there was a good enough case to go for trial.'

So, in spite of Lever's cursing, the Penny Vincent case was added to the indictment and he found himself in the dock at Worcester on all three murders.

Privately, the police, the DPP and the prosecuting counsel knew they hadn't got a hope in hell of a conviction on the first two, but they had added them to the charge to bolster up the only possible winner, that for the killing of Molly Freeman.

This time, all the facts that showed the similarity between the three crimes were being led in evidence and, in his opening speech, Barnes Campbell stressed to the jury the fact that they must not look at each case in isolation, but take all the evidence as parts of a complex whole.

John Hardy sat on his hard seat and listened with absolute concentration. This was probably the most complicated medico-legal case he had ever heard, with three deaths and peculiar features in all of them which made it a kind of forensic crossword puzzle.

The mother stepped down from the witness box and, while the next person was being called, Hardy turned his head to look up at the impassive figure of Lever sitting in the brass-railed dock. He showed not the slightest emotion and Hardy's gaze moved back to Saul Bannerman. He wondered what tricks the lawyer had up his sleeve, to make Lever so unconcerned and apparently confident of the outcome.

Hardy put his hands on the old wood of the desk in

front of him, looking, as he had done a score of times before, at the ancient cracks in the wood, the pits dug by generations of nervous fingernails in the dark brown veneer of wax polish. *If that wood could speak*, he thought, *what tales of horror and misery could it tell – and how many death sentences had passed across it to how many doomed men in the dock behind him*?

He looked up again to see a pink-faced young policeman enter the box and take his oath. This witness mystified the jury, as he had mystified Hardy some months ago, when he had first heard the story from Sam Partridge. He was a Traffic Division constable from Norton Heath, whose very brief evidence was to the effect that on a certain night, after twelve, he had been patrolling the High Street of Norton Heath in a police car together with Sergeant Baxter, when a man whom he knew to be an employee of the Saracen Club came out of the club and drove away in a manner that suggested to the officer that he was under the influence of alcohol.

He drove after him and 'caused him to halt'. Sergeant Baxter approached the car to request him to take a breathalyser test. He saw an altercation taking place at the window of the car and went to the sergeant's assistance, but before he reached the pair, a scuffle was taking place. They arrested the man and took him back to the police station, where he was charged with abusive behaviour, obscene language and refusing to give a breath test.

As the constable left the witness box, Hardy wondered again what really had taken place that night – it sounded as if the police had been lying in wait for people leaving the Saracen. The officer denied, when cross-examined by Adam Quayle, that the sergeant had provoked the man into an argument.

The jury, the Press and spectators were bemused by this apparent irrelevance in a case of murder. One grizzled Press man said in a pub later that he thought that he must have wandered into the wrong court, but the next witness soon made things clear.

This was Sergeant Baxter, who, unknown to anyone else, was Price's ex-RAF pal from way back.

Hardy heard Baxter repeat the gist of the last policeman's statement, then the prosecuting counsel asked the vital question.

'Sergeant, when the man was charged at the police station, you naturally made him empty his pockets before putting him in the cells for the night.'

'Yes, sir. The usual procedure, making an inventory and preparing a receipt.'

Barnes Campbell wagged a finger at a gowned court usher who hovered around the base of the witness box.

'Let the witness see that packet, will you. This will be Exhibit Seven, My Lord.' He raised his head and his voice, as he addressed the red-robed judge.

Mr Justice Wilmott nodded over his cut-away spectacles.

'Now then, Sergeant Baxter, do you recognise those photographs?'

Baxter made a play of pulling two photos from the transparent envelope and looked at them with slightly exaggerated care.

'Yes, sir. These were amongst the effects of the man charged.'

'Bloody liar!'

Suddenly there was a harsh voice from the dock behind Hardy.

His Lordship lowered his head to throw an icy glance across the heads of those in the well of the court.

'Be quiet, will you,' he said evenly, but with an edge to his voice that would have scratched armoured glass.

Both Bannerman and Quayle turned to scowl ferociously at Lever, who sat as motionless as before.

Campbell continued, ignoring the interruption.

'Those photographs are of an exceptionally offensive nature, are they not?'

'Very much so, sir.'

Baxter kept a deadpan expression on his face.

'Did you recognise anyone in the photographs?'

'I did. One was the accused and the other was the dead girl, Molly Freeman.'

The judge leaned across towards the witness box.

'Let me see those, please.'

The elderly court usher almost fell over himself hurrying to convey the packet to the judge, who stared at them with undisguised distaste.

Barnes Campbell watched his face carefully.

'I regret, My Lord, that it is necessary to inflict such material upon the jury. But many of the aspects of this case are equally offensive, I am afraid.'

Mr Justice Wilmott made a face as if he had just taken a dose of senna pods and motioned the usher to take the packet to the jury.

Counsel for the prosecution returned to the witness. 'How did you know who the girl was?'

Baxter, a big, heavily-built man, looked virtuous.

'I'd seen the poster and police notices carrying a photograph of the dead girl, sir. I recognised her at once.'

'And what did you do with the photographs?'

'I immediately brought them to the notice of Detective Inspector Williams, sir. He came in for another purpose later that night.'

Price, up in the gallery, put a hand to his face to cover up a broad smile. *Good old Jack Baxter. He was always a good conman.* Price remembered him back in Aden years ago, persuading a gullible corporal clerk that a goat dung poultice was a sure cure for a wart on his face.

Adam Quayle made some half-hearted attempts to make Baxter admit that he had provoked the arrested man into a quarrel so that he could arrest him. He also started to insinuate that Baxter had planted the photographs in the man's belongings, but a protest from Barnes Campbell stopped him. There was little point in pursuing the matter, as the photographs were genuine beyond any shadow of doubt and it did not much matter how they came to light – the damage had already been done. Hardy found the whole episode a bit hard to swallow.

Price, whose philosophy in life was that the end justifies the means, had another private grin as he looked down on Hardy's neat head below him. He wondered what sort of apoplectic fit Hardy would have if he knew that his own technician had been the catalyst for this whole affair. Then he looked around the gallery and saw that Dickie Durrant and the barman from the Saracen were sitting a few seats away. *Just as well that I'm leaving for London soon*, thought Price.

At lunchtime, the various groups involved in the trial congregated in the hotels and bars of the centre of Worcester. Hardy took Price along with him to have a scratch lunch at a nearby pub, where they found the senior police officers and Archie Salmon already sampling the beer and bar snacks.

The lounge bar was quickly filling up, but they managed to find a corner table and soon a 'mini-trial' was going on around the tankards, pork pies and Cornish pasties. No doubt other similar discussions were going on in other pubs amongst the other factions.

'You're our champion this afternoon, Doc,' muttered Alice over the rim of a pint of Worthington. 'For God's sake come up to your proof, or we're sunk.'

Archie's hairy eyebrows lifted. 'I thought we were home and dry after that little lot this morning ... all that stuff about the dirty pictures?'

Lewis Carrol bit savagely into a slice of pie. 'I don't know so much,' he grunted. 'The jury must have felt that it was all a bit bloody fishy, the way those photos turned up.

And how the others were found.'

'An aggrieved girlfriend, what else?' suggested Archie Salmon.

Hardy, who was confining himself to one shandy, as he had to go into the witness box in an hour, thought back to the last evidence that morning.

'Decidedly odd, that anonymous letter,' he said thoughtfully. 'Firstly, two photographs are found in the pocket of an employee of Lever's who vehemently denies knowing anything about them. Then, within hours of Lever's arrest, a letter arrives telling you to look in his bedside cabinet, where you find a whole stack more!'

Sam Partridge hunched his big shoulders. 'No skin off our noses, Doc. We didn't plant those pictures, did we? If we'd found them in the first place, we'd just have shouted "alleluia" and put them straight in evidence. Like Archie says, the only person who would know about dirty pictures, would have been some bird that Lever had been messing about with, in that bedroom.'

Hardy shook his head slowly. 'It still has a smell to it. I've never heard anything like it in all the time I've been in this business.'

'It got him into the dock, surely that's the main thing,' said Price, smugly. 'It gave the lie to him saying that he'd never heard of Molly Freeman ... and established how fond he is of tying up girls.'

Lewis Carrol washed down his pie with some ale. 'What's this old fox Sir Glanville what's-his-name going to pull out of the hat, I wonder? Is there anything he can stump you on, Doc?'

Hardy sighed. 'Nothing legitimate, that I can think of, Mr Carrol. But going on his form at the magistrates' court some months back, he's liable to come out with the most outrageous statements and get away with it just by his complete lack of sensitivity.'

Price kept his head down over his lunch, to hide the

complacency at seeing his plan come off to perfection. As soon as his pal Baxter had engineered the planting of the two photographs, Price had sent a letter by first-class mail, made up of letters cut from newspaper headlines. It spelt out the fact that the police might be interested to see what 'that bastard Lever' had hidden in his bedside cupboard.

All the photographs, including the two planted ones, carried Lever's fingerprints on the high gloss paper. Price had worn gloves that night, so had no fear of becoming involved himself, though even that would have been highly unlikely, as his prints were nowhere in civilian records.

The lunchtime raced by and soon Hardy found himself back in court, waiting for the judge to return. He was the first witness that afternoon and he could see the beanpole figure of Glanville West in earnest conversation with Adam Quayle. No doubt they were priming the guns to fire at him in cross-examination, but Hardy had not the slightest qualms about that. It was the unknown possibilities that the defence might produce like a jack-in-the-box in a day or two, that caused him most concern.

The judge made his august appearance into court and the afternoon began. Hardy was sworn in by the tailcoated judge's associate and then Barnes Campbell led him through his evidence concerning the death of Molly Freeman. It took some forty minutes for him to relate the reasons why he felt she had been suffocated by something placed over the face, that the stab wounds were inflicted after death and to describe the signs of the sexual attack.

After this, the prosecutor led him fairly quickly through the main points of the post-mortem on the other two girls, concentrating on the common features of sexual activities, tying of the wrists and the plastic bag and asphyxia features.

Then Campbell sat down and the fleshy figure of Adam Quayle hauled itself to its feet.

He threw his black gown back in a theatrical gesture and placed his hands across his waistcoat. He looked not at Hardy, but at the jury on the opposite side of the court. In a loud voice, he began.

'I put it to you, Dr Hardy, that your evidence of suffocation is utterly unfounded and that this girl died from stab wounds.'

There was a silence and Price, looking down from the public gallery, saw his chief collecting his thoughts. *That's it, boy, don't rush into anything, take your time and poke that fat old sod right in the eye.* He willed this at Hardy across the court.

John Hardy, skilled in hundreds of such encounters, needed no telepathic advice.

'My opinion is founded on consideration of the facts, an assessment of possible alternatives and an experience of almost thirty years,' he said mildly.

Adam Quayle tried the thunder and lightning tactics that had largely gone out of date years ago, with such belligerent advocates as Edward Marshall Hall.

'Do you mean to stand there and tell me, Doctor,' he snapped, 'that a woman with four stab wounds in her chest and nothing else to show did not die of those wounds!'

Hardy looked back at him with a slight air of distaste.

'I do indeed,' he said carefully. 'And it is a distortion of the facts to allege that there was nothing else present.

The judge, who himself was a quiet man by nature, leaned forward.

'Mr Quayle, this witness said earlier that he found congestion of the face and lungs and small haemorrhages suggestive of asphyxia. Would you like the shorthand reader to repeat that part of his evidence?'

Quayle, who knew damn fine what Hardy had said earlier, backed off and set out on a new tack.

For an hour, he worried at every point of Hardy's evidence, like a terrier with a rat. He got nowhere at all with the post-mortem evidence as Hardy firmly, politely, but inflexibly, parried every challenge. He had no need to tackle Hardy on the time of death, as between the hours of ten o'clock and one in the morning, Monty Lever had an alibi from two of his men – one of them, the man who had been found with the photographs in his pocket.

By four o'clock, he had finished with Hardy and had made so little impact on his evidence that Barnes Campbell felt no need for a re-examination, which was sometimes necessary, to repair the damage done by a successful cross- examination.

Hardy returned to his seat and looked along the row to where the angular figure of the old ex-India professor sat staring fixedly at the judge. Ever since the man had offended Hardy at the mortuary, months ago, he had never so much as acknowledged Hardy's existence and would walk past him without a word.

The evidence went on with accounts from police officers of Lever's movements, of Archie Salmon's forensic evidence, of descriptions of searches in Lever's flat and witnesses to prove that Lever had associated with Joyce Daniels and Penny Vincent.

The court finished for the day just before five o'clock and Hardy drove Price back home to Warwick.

'What's the chances, Doc?' asked the technician.

'Hard to say. Our side have got a lot of material, but it's all circumstantial.'

'But those photographs. They'll sink him, surely?'

'I don't know. You can know a girl and have sex with her, but that doesn't prove you killed her.'

'But Lever denied ever having heard of her.'

'They'll say he was afraid of getting involved.'

Price was silent. It seemed much easier to commit a murder and get away with it, than to ride a bike without lights or fiddle a quid off the Income Tax.

'Seems flaming crazy to me,' he grunted. 'You've got a

chap who knew all three girls, he's a known kinky sex maniac, semen of his group is in all three – and yet this is the second bloody trial and you reckon he's still a fair chance of getting off!'

Hardy watched the road unfolding beyond the windscreen.

'That's the way of British justice, Price.'

'Justice! What about the poor flaming girls? And the cost of all this police and court palaver? Must have cost thousands so far. If it was up to me, I'd stick him against the wall and shoot him.'

Hardy smiled wanly. 'Then thank heavens it's not up to you, my dear chap. Fellow called Hitler had that sort of idea – and Stalin and Mussolini. But it didn't catch on, for some reason.'

Price sat scowling. *Silly old fool*, he thought. *He would cloud the issue with irrelevances. When a guy is as transparently guilty as Lever, why go through all this rigmarole, with the danger that some fat slug of a lawyer will get him off through some legal loophole?*

When they got home, he sulked a bit, then went down to the King's Head to talk it over again with Charlie Baxter.

Two days later, Professor Sir Glanville West was on the witness stand.

Hardy sat rather tensely, wondering what on earth the old boy was going to come out with this time.

The tall, bony figure stood erect in the box, the same light grey tropical suit falling in drooping folds from his angular shoulders. He had discarded the flower from his lapel, but wore a rather brightly coloured striped tie, which Hardy failed to recognise as any well-known school, college or regiment.

His snow-white hair and full moustache made him a commanding figure and it was quite understandable that anything he said would have quite an impression on a jury.

Adam Quayle rose to lead his witness through his paces. His manner was carefully respectful, calculated to emphasise the renown of this old gentleman.

Price, gazing down from his commanding position, also noticed the difference in Quayle's manner.

'Good as called the boss a flaming liar,' he said to himself. 'But he's kowtowing to this old fossil just to con the jury.'

Quayle went through all Glanville West's qualifications and all of his appointments, again in a reverential manner. Hardy tapped Barnes Campbell on the shoulder and leaned forward.

'Not a single one of those is medico-legal or forensic,' he whispered in his ear.

The prosecution counsel nodded and scribbled something on his large blue notebook.

Quayle went on to make as much of a meal as possible about West's attendance to perform a second post-mortem examination.

'And what, Professor, was your opinion as to the cause of death?'

The old doctor drew himself up to yet another slender inch and placed his blue-veined hands on the edge of the witness box.

'Stab wounds to the chest, of course,' he declared in a high voice.

Adam Quayle flapped his gown about him like the wings of an old raven.

'You don't agree with Dr John Hardy's ideas on the subject?'

Sir Glanville West turned his pale blue eyes on the jury.

'Indeed I do not. It seems transparently obvious that someone who has been stabbed four times in the chest died from this!'

Hardy groaned, but quietly. He did not like to show his

exasperation for a colleague in public.

'And the signs that Dr Hardy took for asphyxia, you discount?'

West bobbed his head rapidly. 'I have looked at numerous microscopic sections of the lungs. They show congestion ...' He launched into a long description which was as relevant to the matter in hand as if he had been describing the rivets in the hull of the *QEII*.

John Hardy felt his blood pressure going up several notches, but his time had not yet come and all he could do was to sit and scribble furious notes to pass to Barnes Campbell in front.

Eventually, Quayle sat down with a triumphant flourish and the less flamboyant Campbell rose to his feet. He was a big man, but large in a craggy, rugby-style way, not the podgy flab of the defence QC.

He arranged his papers and blue notebook precisely on the little lectern in front of him.

'Professor West, what forensic appointments have you held?'

The old man's watery eyes swivelled round the court and came back to Campbell.

'Forensic? I am a pathologist, sir. An emeritus professor of pathology.'

'Quite so. But will you please answer the question?'

This brought the professor up short.

'No specific appointments, but. a pathologist is a pathologist, forensic or not.'

'I would differ with that, sir, and so would many pathologists, said Campbell calmly. 'But, tell me, how many murder post-mortems have you conducted?'

The man from India hummed and hawed, but was eventually pinned down to saying that he had done several dozen.

'In forty-five years? That doesn't seem very many, compared with the hundreds that have comprised Dr

Hardy's experience.'

Gradually, Campbell peeled off the layers of Glanville West's alleged compendious knowledge of legal medicine, then moved to more specific matters.

'You say that Molly Freeman died of stab wounds … in that case, how do you explain that a half-inch wound in her aorta, the main blood vessel in the body, failed to produce torrential bleeding?'

Hardy began to feel sympathy for the old man in the box. He himself had known the feeling of being destroyed in front of a court full of people. Even the knowledge that West had brought it on himself did not allay the embarrassment that began to well up, along with the sympathy.

'Er … she was already dead.'

'From what … asphyxia?'

'No, no, no …'

He sounded testy, even as he was sinking.

'The stab that cut the aorta was the last wound. She was already dead from one of the previous three.'

Barnes Campbell smiled benignly at the jury.

'That's very interesting,' he said smoothly. 'And how do you know it was the last wound?'

'Er … well, I'm surmising it.'

'Exactly. On no evidence, you are surmising it. Now, we have heard that none of the other three stab wounds penetrated any vital structure whatsoever. So, of what did she die, if it was due to one of those?'

Glanville West agitatedly dragged out his monocle from his jacket pocket and polished it vigorously, to give himself time to think.

'Er … shock. Must have been shock! Vagal inhibition, in fact.'

Campbell adjusted his book again.

'Vagal inhibition. That's a term I thought had vanished from the textbooks, and the courts, many years ago. Now

185

tell us, Professor, how did you arrive at this diagnosis of death from shock?'

West woofled again and screwed his monocle into his wrinkled face.

'Well, by exclusion. Four stab wounds. Shock.'

Barnes Campbell studied another note from Hardy.

'When people die of this rather mysterious shock, Professor, what are the appearances?'

'Well, none. Nothing specific, that is.'

'Are they not usually pale? Does not the heart stop suddenly?'

'It stops suddenly, yes.'

'Molly Freeman was very congested. She had tiny haemorrhages in her eyes and on the surface of her very congested lungs, which you so exhaustively described a few minutes ago. Is that what you would expect in your "shock", Professor?'

His voice had gradually increased in volume as he spoke, until the last words were uttered in a crescendo.

Hardy felt like crawling under the bench. Although it was his legitimate advice that had made the bullets for Barnes Campbell to fire, he hated seeing the old chap being shot down in flames.

Up in the gallery, Price had no such inhibitions and he grinned evilly as Glanville West muttered some ineffectual reply. In fact, Price had to restrain himself from a round of applause. But, apart from the certainty of being ejected by the court ushers, the sight of a group of Monty Lever's pals in the row behind was a completely effective deterrent.

That evening, Price and Hardy stood in the laboratory of the house. It was piled high with wooden crates, some already nailed down, others spewing shavings and corrugated cardboard over the floor.

Part of the consignment was being picked up by the

removers on the next day; the rest of the household furniture was due to be shifted to Marlow on Friday.

'Any more to go in this one?' asked Price, checking the contents of a large box against a list on a clipboard.

'No, you can screw that one down, please,' said Hardy absently.

He was still thinking of the day's events in the Crown Court. Partly, it was a defence against the sight of one part of his life being folded up, as if it had never happened. This was the room where he had investigated so many cases, where Jo had talked to him about so many of them, and had helped him when things were tough.

He wondered what she would have made of the Lever affair, one of the oddest and least satisfactory of all his career.

'Doc … I said what about this?'

Price had been talking to him, but he had been far away, at least in time.

'Er, sorry, I was daydreaming.'

Price, though outwardly a cynical and unromantic character, knew fine what was going on in his boss's head.

'Bit of a wrench, I suppose. How long have you been here?'

'In this particular house? Oh, about eighteen years. It's a long time, Price.'

'Moving keeps you young. You'll be a new man in Marlow, you watch. All that London life … you'll have a sports car and suede shoes before you know where you are.'

Hardy smiled at Price. In a few months, he had developed a peculiar bond with this odd, amoral man. They were utterly unlike, yet the differences seemed to dovetail, rather than clash. Price was a foil for him to fence with – and perhaps a bit of an abrasive on which to sharpen his wits.

He looked around at the shambles that was once his

immaculate laboratory.

'I can't stand it anymore. Let's give it up. The removal men should be doing this, anyway – they're charging enough.'

Hardy went into the kitchen and switched on the electric kettle. His daily woman, her job almost finished, had left a tray with the makings of coffee and they sat down to have a drink.

'What's this girl like, the one that's going to be your secretary down in Marlow?' asked Price.

'Her name is Susan. She's not actually going to be my secretary, but more a research assistant. Like you, this grant from Vinton College is going to pay her. I want someone who can grub around in the university libraries and get out papers and references for the bone project.'

Price mulled this over.

'Is she a "miss" or a "missus"?'

Hardy smiled at him. 'Jumping ahead a bit, eh, Price. Actually, she's a "missus". A divorcee, so I understand from her letter.'

Price groaned. 'Some hardbitten battleaxe of about fifty-five, I'll bet.'

'She's in her thirties, as it happens. And the bank manager she gave as a reference told me on the telephone that she's a very smart, attractive woman.'

Price gave him a knowing wink.

'Watch your step, Doc. Divorcees are the worst.'

John Hardy tried to crush him with a cold stare, but somehow it turned into a twisted grin.

'Worry about yourself, Price. You're an eligible bachelor, too.'

Next day, the Lever case reached its climax. The rest of the defence witnesses went into the witness box to 'perjure themselves stupid about Monty Lever's alibi', as Lewis Carrol said bitterly.

Three men, including Dickie Durrant, the manager of the Saracen Club, swore that, between them, they could account for every minute of Lever's time from six o'clock that evening until two thirty the next morning.

Their alibi evidence carefully overlapped the vital period each side of midnight, so that they corroborated each other. Nothing that Barnes Campbell could say could shake the simple claim that Lever had been with them all the time. There was no other witness besides these three to substantiate their story, but as the Crown had no one at all to deny the evidence, by proving that the owner had been anywhere else during that period, the suspect evidence of the three became better than the completely negative claims of the prosecution.

After all the witnesses had been heard, the two eminent Queen's Counsel got up to make their closing speeches. Both were excellent in their differing ways.

Campbell was dry, straightforward, but impressive by his directness and his beautiful voice.

Adam Quayle made more use of his acting talents and his histrionic abilities. It was obvious that the medical evidence had fallen flat on its face as far as the defence was concerned.

Hardy had come out on top and Sir Glanville West, who had vanished from the court, had been routed to the last degree.

Hardy felt satisfied at last that the criticisms that had been levelled at him over the past few months were now swept under the carpet for good. However, he felt that he could never resume his previous relations with James Donnington after the attitude that the Dean of the Faculty had taken, even though it had been proved utterly unjustified.

The main gist of the prosecution's submission to the jury was that here was a series of killings, all virtually identical in method, all with evidence of perverted sexual practices and all associated with a man with the same blood group. They pointed the finger at Monty Lever, who had known each girl, had denied knowing one of them, and who obviously had the same sexual perversion as the killer. All logical and circumstantial, but lacking any positive physical connection between the man, his car and his home and the dead girls.

On the other side, Hardy heard Adam Quayle expertly and persuasively invite the jury to wonder how the accused could *possibly* have done what he was alleged to have done, when he was in the company of three men all the time. And he reminded the twelve jurors that not a shred of evidence had been found to connect the girls with Lever. No fingerprints, no fibres, no bloodstains – nothing.

He rattled off a string of well-known cases from the past, where circumstantial evidence had been proved wrong. He dinned into their minds the ghastly responsibility they had of possibly sending an innocent man to prison, because a chain of coincidences told against him.

As he listened, John Hardy had a great deal of reluctant admiration for Quayle's ingenuity and eloquence, but Price became more and more angry that such an open-and-shut case should be so expertly whitewashed, that the jury might end up giving Lever a medal.

In the early afternoon, the jury went out, after hearing the final word from the judge, who summed up in an admirably fair way that left absolutely no bias one way or the other. What he said, in dignified legal terms, was in effect 'You pays your money and you takes your choice!' They were to take until the afternoon of the next day to make up their minds.

The phone rang and Hardy stretched a hand out of bed to answer it. It couldn't be a police call, as he was moving today, going away for ever.

But it was – at least, it was Lewis Carrol on the other end. Hardy looked sleepily at the bedside clock. It said seven twenty-five, just coming up to breakfast time.

'It's a little early, Chief Superintendent,' he murmured, rubbing his eyes.

'I knew you were moving today. I thought I'd better get you before you got too involved. Have you heard about Monty Lever?'

Hardy's jaw tightened.

'Naturally, it was on the local radio and in the late editions of the papers last night. A great disappointment, but not altogether a surprise.'

Alice sounded unusually excited.

'No, no, not about his acquittal by that mentally defective jury.'

Hardy sat upright in bed. 'What are you talking of, then?'

'Lever ... he's in hospital! Be there for a couple of months.'

John Hardy tried to make sense of what Lewis Carrol was saying.

'But he seemed perfectly all right in court yesterday. Has the shock of being acquitted given him a coronary or something?'

Alice almost yelled down the phone.

'Better than that! He went out to celebrate last night, got pretty high at the Saracen with all his perjuring cronies. He drove himself home to Knowle, left his car in the road outside his flat and before he could reach his front door, somebody hit him for six with a car.'

John Hardy swung himself on the edge of the bed and shuffled his feet around to find his slippers.

'Was it an accident or deliberate?'

'Don't know! Sounds like a hit-and-run, but the chances of accidentally knocking down one person on a deserted road at three in the morning seem decidedly bloody slight. Especially when that one person is a twisted villain who has just wriggled out of a murder charge.'

'Extraordinary! Any prospect of tracing the vehicle?'

'Not much. No tyre marks, though somebody in the flats heard a screech of brakes and a skid. No paint from the vehicle on the road nor on Lever's clothes.'

'Is he badly injured?'

'No fear of him passing away, unfortunately.' Lewis Carrol sounded disappointed. 'But he's got umpteen fractures that'll keep him in hospital for a month and in plaster for three, so they say. Thought I'd let you know ... natural justice, so to speak.'

'God moves in mysterious ways,' agreed Hardy solemnly.

Alice grunted. 'More likely some aggrieved girlfriend, rather than the Almighty. Or perhaps the boyfriend of a girl – one who felt the same as I do about yesterday's miscarriage of justice.'

'But you didn't take a motor car to him,' commented Hardy.

When he had put the phone down, he slipped on his dressing gown and went into the kitchen. He heard Price searching for cups in the packing case which held the china.

'I've had an extraordinary piece of news, Price ...' he began.

Then he stopped, for he saw that Price had a large bruise on his forehead and a bloodstained sticking plaster along one eyebrow. As he moved back to the sink with the cups, he limped heavily on his left foot.

'What on earth happened to you?' said Hardy, alarmed.

Price dumped the crockery in the sink and turned the hot tap on them.

'I fell off my bike,' he said.

The Sixties Mysteries
by
Bernard Knight

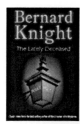   

The Lately Deceased
The Thread of Evidence
Mistress Murder
Russian Roulette
Policeman's Progress
Tiger at Bay
The Expert

For more information about **Bernard Knight**
and other **Accent Press** titles
please visit

www.accentpress.co.uk

Lightning Source UK Ltd.
Milton Keynes UK
UKOW02f0315250316

270833UK00001BC/13/P